A DREAM THAT LASTED NINE CENTURIES

MILENA ORLIC-KOVACIC

authorHOUSE®

AuthorHouse™ UK
1663 Liberty Drive
Bloomington, IN 47403 USA
www.authorhouse.co.uk
Phone: 0800.197.4150

Published by AuthorHouse   04/09/2019

ISBN: 978-1-7283-8375-0 (sc)
ISBN: 978-1-7283-8725-3 (hc)
ISBN: 978-1-7283-8374-3 (e)

AUTHOR'S NOTE

This book is not a history.

This book is a novel based on diaries, and all personalities and events are imagined.

Any similarity with real people or real events is coincidental.

CONTENTS

PROLOGUE

Professor Vojković was asleep. He could hear drums pounding somewhere faraway, but they were coming closer and closer. Now somebody was shouting his name.

"Professor Vojković, Professor Vojković, open the door, please."

Slowly, through his dream, he became aware that the voice was coming from the outside. Somebody was banging on his door.

He got up and went to the hall. "Who is it so early?"

"Police. Open the door, please."

"In a minute," he said.

He quickly dressed up and opened the door. "Hello. What's the problem?"

"My name is Georg Varvik," said a tall, slim man. "I'm detective inspector at the police headquarters in Zagreb. Two hours ago, near the lake Jarun, we found a dead man. His name is Maximillian Morgenstern. Does that name mean anything to you?"

"No. Why do you think that I should know him? I've never heard that name."

"The man had a paper in the pocket of his jacket with your name and address on it. Are you sure you don't know anybody by that name?"

"Positive."

"OK, but there is another reason for our visit. Beside him, we found a tablet made of white limestone with text in the Glagolitic script on it. We are informed that you're one of the few people who can read and translate it. So would you, please, come with me?"

"Where are we going?"

"First, to the police morgue to check. Maybe you know the man under a different name. And then to our headquarters to look at that tablet and translate the text."

"A tablet with Glagolitic script etched on it? That's very interesting. Glagolitic is the old Slavic script, and there are just a few monuments with text written in it. The most famous is King Zvonimir's donation. The tablet was found in 1851 in the Church of St Lucy in Jurandvor, on the island of Krk, and it's kept in the Croatian Academy of Sciences and Arts, Zagreb."

The professor rubbed his chin in thought. "Apart from that, there are just a few other donations and statues of their gods, like the statue of the Slavic chief god Perun, the god of the thunder, and the statue of Vesna, Hrvatska's goddess of the spring. Legend says that Perun has three faces: the first face with a gentle, friendly smile; the second serious and worrying; and the third very angry, with lightning all around. Yes, I will gladly come with you. I'm very interested."

After these words, he grabbed his coat and hat and stepped out of the apartment to join the inspector.

At the morgue, the professor looked at the dead body. He noticed a number on the man's right arm. "No, never saw him," he said. "But what about that number? Doesn't that help you?"

"Yes, we saw that," Inspector Detective Georg Varvik said. "We know that is significant. We already got his name and surname thanks to that number, but for now, it tells us nothing except that the man was in a concentration camp.

At the headquarters, the inspector gave Professor Vojković the tablet. The first thing Vojković noticed was that the tablet didn't have any archaeological value—it had been made recently. He was surprised, but he kept that to himself. He wondered who had made it. The only person he could think of was his neighbour Stella. She was an archaeologist and a specialist in Slavic tribes, including their habits and culture. But he wondered what the reason could be. And more important, what was her connection with the dead man?

Aloud he said, "The translation is, 'Only one is left.' The man was killed—poisoned—and this message can only mean that there will be at least one more dead body in the future. And that there were murdered people in the past as well."

"Well, better something than nothing," said the inspector. "Can we count on your help if something new shows up?"

"Certainly. I'm very interested to learn what this is all about."

But police didn't find anything more. They checked archives in Zagreb and browsed through Interpol's archive in Paris, but they found nothing. They wrote "Unsolved" on the folder and archived it.

Two months later, the inspector called the professor again. "Something new showed up in our case. In an old, abandoned building, children found two big, fat books with strange writing. They talked about the books all the time, trying to solve the significance of their findings. The father of one of the kids is a police officer. He overheard them talking about books. He remembered all that excitement a few months ago and immediately called me. For us, this case stays unsolved. The tablet and the books are in the museum. I was hoping that you could take some free time to run through those books. Maybe you will find something interesting—a clue, or maybe even the solution."

Professor Vojković was thrilled. He went to the museum. Custos, the director, was glad to see him and was very interested as well.

Vojković opened the first page and read.

> Those two books are about Hrvats immigrating
> to the Balkan Peninsula and their fight to survive.
> All events that happened before the ninth century
> were like fairy tales: hard to believe. They're full
> of stories about fighting with fierce animals and
> the forces of nature. Stories about heroes, about
> young knights who were protecting the weak.
> That book is called …

CHAPTER 1

LEGEND

This part of my diary is based on the old people's stories. We have a habit, during the long winter nights, to sit beside the fire and talk about the past. Those stories were told so many times, from so many different people, with something being added and something being left out, that it was impossible to separate the truth from the imagination.

I will try to present those stories the best I remember.

It was a small tribe—just around two thousand men, women, and children. They lived in a canyon in a country called Snowy Mountain. The tribe was called Hrvati, and they were part of a bigger group called White Hrvati. Their main occupation was tending livestock, but they were skilled and brave warriors as well.

Their land was nice. They had many green meadows with enough grass for their animals—for the time being. But they knew that soon they would need more space. Around them were thick forests with enough wood to build their houses.

Through the middle of the canyon ran a river full of fish.

This sounds idyllic, but life was very hard. The winters were harsh, and there were many wild animals in the forests—bears, wolfs, and foxes. These wild animals frequently attacked sheep, chickens, and the bigger animals like cows and horses. They even attacked people.

Although these Hrvats were excellent hunters, life there was a challenge.

So long ago, when our story starts, the ruler of the tribe was Myron, who lived from about 680 until 735.

Myron had very simple laws for fighting crime and punishing criminals. For the thieves, if they were caught—and they usually were—they had to work for the affected party without pay for as long as was needed to repay the value of the stolen goods.

For murderers, the penalty was death.

Violent people were banished.

Every case was decided by solid evidence, and logical conclusions had to be given to the three judges chosen by Myron. His decision was final.

One winter, an old nomad came into their village. They gave him a roof over his head and fed him through the winter. They shared bread and salt with him, meaning they were now friends, and he tried to entertain them with stories about the places he'd seen and the people he'd met. He described beautiful places, including the dense forests; lovely, peaceful lakes; and wild rivers. He described the dangerous places, including the tall mountains always under snow with the danger of avalanches.

He talked about the friendly tribes and not-so-friendly tribes.

But he talked the most about the place called the Balkan far down on the southern, warm, sunny coast of the blue Adriatic Sea. He told them that the place was like heaven. The only problem was Avars regularly attacked local inhabitants, killing them and stealing their livestock.

In the spring, the old man was gone, and they were left to think about that promised land. They decided, after lots of discussion and arguing, that they should go to the Balkan.

Their present country was beautiful but small. They needed a much bigger space. They needed the new land.

"Whoever wants to stay is free to stay. The decision is completely yours. Whoever wants to go, let's get moving."

That was the final decision.

They performed the usual procedures for their gods, asking for their blessing. Then they packed the necessary gear and prepared the livestock for the trek.

Finally, the big movement to the south started. They travelled for months, crossing rivers and climbing mountains. On their way, they met lots of other tribes; it was a time of migration for tribes all over Europe, including Gauls, Goths, Franks, and Vandals. Lots of them joined the Hrvats' little group and continued with them. Instead of around 1,500 people, it was 20,000 coming to Dalmatia.

After three months, they finally reached the Balkan. Upon passing through Gorski Kotar, they climbed the mountain called Risnyak, and in the distance through the mist, they saw the blue Adriatic. That was a magnificent view. They realised that this would be hard to conquer and keep. But when they saw it, it looked like it was waiting for them. They knew they would get it and keep it. And they did.

They settled in the area between Rijeka and Zadar.[1] Soon they found out that in that part of the world, there already existed one province called Hrvatska Pannonia under the rule of the Frankish emperor. These two regions (provinces) had existed while separated through the centuries.

Hrvatska made an agreement with Illyrians and the emperor of the country of Byzantine, Heraclius. "We will protect and defend the borders and the local inhabitants— Illyrians—in return for the permission to immigrate."

Avars tried to continue with old tactic—making quick raids, killing people, and stealing flocks—but they couldn't break through the defending wall of Hrvatska's warriors. After a few years of unsuccessful attempts, they decided to stop with the attacks, keep the land they already had, and live in peace.

Hrvatska was growing. The tribes who inhabited the land around it joined Hrvatska and accepted its language, culture,

---

[1] Cities on the Adriatic coast.

and traditions. In just fifteen years, Hrvatska's country covered the Adriatic coast from Hrvatska's Primorje to Dubrovnik with the exception of the few islands.

After Myron's death, the new ruler was chosen between the ten strongest members of the tribe. His name was Zdravomir (736–790). He chose Novigrad as his capital city, and in Novigrad he built his fortress.

After the death of Zdravomir, the new ruler was his daughter Vesna (named after the goddess of spring). Vesna was a very good governor, and her people loved and respected her. She was a widow and had two girls under her care, including her own daughter

Zoya was beautiful, very gentle, shy, and blonde-haired. Her younger sister, Nevena, was a skilled, intelligent, gorgeous brunette who was a master in fencing and archery. She looked like Diane, the Roman goddess of hunting, was always in a good humour, and was very popular.

Unfortunately, Byzantine Emperor Heraclius decided to visit his provinces accompanied by ten soldiers for protection. The commander of the soldiers was a man called Rudolph Mintz. The moment he saw Nevena, he decided that she must be his. He followed her and approached her with ambiguous compliments, being real nuisance. She didn't know how to get rid of him.

However, one day he approached her and said, "Listen, Nevena. You are well-known as a master in fencing, you can compete, and you are the only woman who's allowed to partake in the knights' games. You are the winner in the competitions, but I don't believe that you are so good. I think that lads like you, and they let you win. Compete with me. You choose the weapon. If I win, you will be mine. If you win, I will never bother you again."

She accepted the challenge because she was fed up with his behaviour, and if this contest would get rid of the undesirable admirer, so be it. She didn't have any doubt that she would win.

Rudolph continued. "We won't tell anybody about that. We will simply go to the park, by the statue of your pagan god Perun; he will be the only witness." She agreed with that and didn't say a word to anybody, not even to her sister.

The next morning, they met in the park. Nevena chose the sword. Rudolph believed that this would be an easy victory. He thought, *What can this woman know about fencing? She is just a spoilt fool.* However, he was surprised by the skill and the force of her attacks, and he decided to surrender before he got hurt.

"Stop, stop. I give up. I must admit that you're better in fencing then me. You won." When she stopped, he said, "Fair Nevena, with your skills, you're sure to stay an old maid forever. Let's have a drink to put the dot on this case."

"I don't drink," she said.

"Oh, please, take just one sip, and then you won't see me or hear about me ever again." She wasn't looking at him and didn't notice the crooked smile on his face when he said that.

"OK, just one sip," she said as took the drink.

After drinking, she felt her body stiffen—she couldn't move. She was drugged.

"OK, boys, you can come out now," said Rudolph. "We will sacrifice this virgin to her God."

After those words, he ripped off her clothes and raped her.

It was snowing, and snowflakes fell on Perun's face. They melted there, turning into water. It looked like the old god was crying.

When Rudolph finished, he turned toward his friends and said, "It's your turn now."

But they had had time to cool down, and they were suddenly aware of the crime they'd nearly committed due to the euphoria of Rudolph's constant pushing. They would be severely punished even if she was a little peasant girl—and she was the princess. They turned and left that place, leaving him alone.

Rudolph extended his hand to reach the sword again, but he stopped and froze when he saw the big wolf coming from behind Perun's statue. Then he started running, but the wolf didn't follow him; it instead cuddled beside Nevena, keeping her warm.

At sundown, Nevena tried to move. The effect of the drug was gone, and she slowly regained her strength and mobility. When she thought she was strong enough, she started the long, painful walk home with the wolf following her at a short distance. She was covered with blood and mud; she looked like a beast followed by another beast. Finally, she reached her home, opened the front yard's gate, and stepped in.

Servants started screaming. "Monster! Monster!"

Vesna came out to see what was happening. Nevena stepped towards Vesna and fainted. Servants gathered around her. Her face, washed by rain, was now clearly visible. They recognised her.

Vesna screamed, "Nevena! Nevena! What's happened?"

Nevena opened her eyes and said, "He raped me!" Then she fainted again.

With the help of her servants, Vesna quickly brought Nevena into the house and rushed around her, removing wet and ripped clothes. She cleaned all the injuries with rakija,[2] put some herbal ointments on the injuries, and then wrapped her sister up in blankets and put her in bed. After that, she sent a messenger to bring her cousins Harmon and Don to her house.

---

[2] An alcoholic drink.

CHAPTER 2

FAMILY OATH

Nevena was now asleep. She had a long and healthy rest. When she woke, she was strong and determined to punish that criminal. She told the members of her family what had happened and then said, "Let's go to Perun's temple."

They followed her without a word. When they reached the temple, they entered and stopped beside Perun 's statue.

Nevena said, "Repeat after me."

> I swear to you, Perun, here and now that I will do all that is in my power to bring this criminal, Rudolph Mintz, to justice. He is a very dangerous criminal because he is able to gather people around him and persuade them to follow him in crime. I swear that I and my descendants will fight and punish everyone like him.

They repeated this oath and turned to go home, but Vesna stopped them. "I have something to add to this oath. please repeat after me."

> I swear that I will do everything possible (and impossible) to protect Hrvatska and make it an independent country.

On the way home, Nevena told them that their oath was a difficult duty because they must act only in a legal way. They would always be in deadly danger because criminals didn't care about the law. Criminals would use every type of weapon and every way of attack without hesitation.

After that, they went home. When they reached the fortress, Vesna was surprised to see a stranger at her house's doorstep. Nevena ran toward him, very excited.

"Invite him in. Vesna, please, that's Almer."

"Who is Almer?" Vesna asked.

"I'll tell you, but first let him in."

He was already in the room and saying, "Nevena! My dear, sweet Nevena, what happened to you? I had horrible dreams. I told to my people to prepare everything for the wedding. I don't take no for an answer to my proposals. I love you, and I know that you love me. What does it matter that you're Hrvat and I am Avar? You're a woman and I'm a man. I love you, you love me, and we're going to get married."

Nevena told him what had happened, and she continued. "You're right. My reason for refusal was the fact that we belong to different tribes. I changed my mind. I honour your proposal, and I will marry you if you still want me."

"Of course, I do. Nothing can change my love."

After that, she told him about their oath, and he said, I will go tomorrow to visit old Perun, and I will repeat your oath. We will be together in everything, in good and in bad."

Here Vesna interrupted. "No Nevena, no! You can't marry Avar! If you marry Avar, how can I persuade Zoya to marry Venice's prince? She's in love with the friend from her childhood, young Appal, but I have different plans with her. Prince Franco Node from Venice proposed, and I accepted in Zoya's name. Hrvatska needs a strong ally, and Venice is God's gift."

"What? You will destroy your child. Please don't do that. She is so gentle, so sensitive. That will kill her. I don't think that Venice is an ally. They want the whole of Dalmatia as well. They are very dangerous enemies because they are secret enemies."

"Sorry," said Vesna. "I've made up my mind!" She exited the room.

Nevena and Almer were left alone to talk about their future actions.

"First the wedding," said Almer.

It took two months before they were ready for the wedding. Nevena needed to recover completely from her injuries.

Rudolph Mintz nearly had a heart attack when he saw her inviting everybody to celebrate her wedding.

"My God. She's alive, and she is more beautiful than ever," he whispered to himself. Then he said to his friends, "We must run and hide, or she will kill us all. What type of woman is she? Another woman would stay hidden in the house, ashamed and scared, but this one is parading around in full glory as if nothing's ever happened to her."

However, his friends decided they didn't have a reason to run—and that they shouldn't be seen in his company. He had to run alone.

The wedding was held in the national park Plitvice, a wonder of nature and beauty. Eighteen lakes surrounded by the green hills, and lakes on the different levels, connected with waterfalls. It was unspeakable perfection and a performance of nature, and it reflected Nevena's adequate appearance. Her wedding dress was white linen of domestic production, and she was adorned with floral motifs of her own handiwork. Her beautiful black hair was made into plaits on the top of her head and covered with a headscarf made in the same way as her dress.

The groom had white linen trousers. The shirt was made like Novena's dress, the waistcoat was made from choha,[3] and he had black hat. They were a gorgeous couple.

Rudolph couldn't resist watching the wedding, but now he knew he must go. He knew her strength. He grabbed a horse and ran out of Plitvice, out of Hrvatska.

Heraclius was long gone after choosing new soldiers from Hrvatska. Vesna said, "Now is time to punish those bandits."

---

[3] Type of fine wool textile; katun.

They were already caught and put in the jail, waiting for trial. They were found guilty of helping the criminal to commit a crime equal to the murder, and the verdict was that Rudolph Mintz would be hanged for rape.

Dushan Marek, the strongest in the group who was holding the princess and making jokes on her account during the criminal act, would be hanged.

The rest of them would be banished from Hrvatska, never to come back.

Vesna informed the emperor about this verdict, and he agreed.

Vesna and the whole family looked for Rudolph. They promised an award in gold for any useful information, but they couldn't find him.

In the meantime, there were urgent preparations for Zoya's wedding. The prince requested three cities (Split, Trogir, and Zadar) from Dalmatia as Zoya's dowry. Vesna tried to escape that part of the contract, but the prince was clear: no cities, no wedding. In the end, Vesna signed the contract as it was. The wedding was held in Venice. Vesna was delighted, but Zoya was devastated.

A few months after Zoya's wedding, Appal showed up in Novigrad's fortress. He approached Vesna with all due respect.

"Madam, Zoya is in a great danger. The prince wanted her just to get hold of these three towns. He is not interested in Zoya or any other woman—he prefers boys. He imprisoned Zoya in the fortress in Senj, but I have a friend there, and he told me that the prince intends to kill Zoya because she knows too much about his crimes.

"We don't have much time. My friend will help me get her out of Senj. Madam, please go to the pope and demand he nullify that marriage as not consummated. I love Zoya and she loves me, but we don't want to live in sin. I want to take her in my home as my bride."

They did as planned, and soon Zoya was home and safe. The Prince kept Split, Zadar, and Trogir. Still, he couldn't get over the fact that he had to let go of Zoya. She was the perfect victim, just the type he liked to torture. He wanted her dead.

On one of his drinking nights rumbling through the streets of Venice, he met Rudolph Mintz. They clicked together perfectly. Prince invited Rudolph in his castle. At first he hesitated, not knowing how to start. Then he said, "I heard you have some problems with those Hrvats?"

"Yes," said Rudolph. "I heard the same about you. What can we do about that?"

"Well," Prince said, "I have a ring." He took a beautiful, very expensive ring from his safe and showed it to Rudolph. This ring has a secret little box hidden under the big green emerald, and on the side of the emerald was a hidden needle with two heads. When somebody tried to put the ring on the finger, the pressure would push the needle in the powder, which was the snake's dried poison, and then pierce the skin. Death was inevitable.

Prince said, "I suggest you to go to Hrvatska and give this ring to my former wife with my apologies for being such as bad husband. Tell her that I am now aware of how good she was and how much I miss her. If she doesn't fall for that and refuses the ring, find another way to get rid of her, but she must die. Keep the ring as a reward for her death. When you finish, go wherever you want to—just keep away from me. We will never meet again."

He very carefully pushed the emerald to the side. There was a little box under it full of white powder, as well as the needle.

Before going to Hrvatska, Rudolph managed to meet his son, Emilio Fabrizio, and told him everything about his task and the ring. He told him where to find the ring and how its mechanism worked in the case he didn't come back in the two weeks. Then Rudolph disguised himself as a woman, took an ordinary needle, and put some of that white powder on it. He hid the ring again and went to Hrvatska.

It was Zoya's wedding day, which was a lovely sunny day. Everybody was out to say goodbye to Zoya and Appal. They were going to live in Appal's country.

Rudolph didn't have any intention of showing up in the castle. He knew that he was sentenced to death. In that moment, he noticed Nevena and decided to kill her, but Nevena noticed him as well.

She looked over her shoulder and saw a suspicious-looking woman. She knew who that was without a second look— she would never forget that eyes. Secretly she gave a sign to the guard on her left side, and he alerted the others. They were dressed as civilians, and Rudolph couldn't see anything suspicious. They were watching his moves, and when they saw his hand coming out of his pocket with the needle in it, they acted very quickly, grabbed him, and arrested him. The investigation was complete and effective. They found his accommodation and lots of plans for an attack on Hrvatska. It was obvious that he was Venice's spy. Somehow, he knew all the weak spots in the defence, all the hidden entries, and all the underground passages in Hrvatska's fortresses.

Rudolph was afraid that they would torture him, and so he confessed that he was working for Venice without waiting to be asked. The investigation was successful. He was found guilty for the rape and treason. The punishment was death by hanging.

When he heard his verdict, he knew that there was no way out, and he started swearing. "You bloody Hrvats! You can kill me, but you can't kill all your enemies. You can't even imagine how many out there want your beautiful country. You can't fight them all!"

He was hanged the very next day.

The wedding passed without any incident.

Zoya and Appal chose to live in Appal's country, and Nevena lived with Almer on the Snowy Mountain.

Nevena and Almer travelled from Snowy Mountain through Europe in a search for spies and criminals. They discovered a net of spies in other countries, Pannonian and Dalmatian Hrvatska, who were working for Hungary and Venice. Both countries were ready to give good money for any useful information.

Nevena and her family were the targets of every criminal organisation around, but they managed to escape the traps and bring the culprits to justice. They had just one child, daughter Philippa. Philippa had two daughters, Yagoda and Hope. Yagoda was ten years older than Hope. When they reached maturity, they both joined their parents and grandparents in their hunts, having the envious success in that important work.

It was in a strange way that Nevena succeeded escaping danger every time.

She had a secret helper. Somebody was leaving warnings about the traps prepared for her and her family. She was the only one who noticed them and was able to make them out. Sometimes there were wild flowers put in the ground in a certain order, which she understood. Sometimes it was a lovely drawing (the person was an artist). Sometimes it was a short letter etched in stone in a script that she knew (Glagolitic). Those messages were her secret, and she didn't say anything to anybody; she didn't want her family laughing at her.

One day she noticed two blue eyes staring at her from the bushes. The eyes were deep blue like the Adriatic Sea, which she loved and admired. Her heart stopped beating for a second when she realised who it was. She didn't do anything but gave a friendly smile as acknowledgement. Happiness lit the little face.

Her family was surprised at how she collected all that strange drawings. When they asked why she did that and whether the tablets had some secret significance, she would simply say that she liked the drawings.

Zoya and Appal were working on destroying evil in their country. They didn't have children, but they often visited Nevena and her family. Vesna was with Zoya most of the time.

As for the prince, Vesna complained to the pope about his behaviour—how he'd treated Zoya and how he'd intended to kill her. The pope was fed up with all the complaints about the prince. He erased him from the lists of nobility, and his properties were taken and given to the church. He became a homeless tramp.

Vesna retired long before that. She let all the dukes rule. Her Hrvatska needed a stronger hand.

However, she was worried. She often thought about Rudolph's last words, and she used every opportunity to remind her family about their oaths, demanding all of them be alert and look out for the people like Rudolph who would destroy them. They should do everything in their power to make Hrvatska independent.

From the moment of Rudolph's death, Vesna realised how wrong she was for thinking that Venice was ally. Her body shivered every time she remembered that table in his room, with all the plans and drawings. Hrvatska was open to the enemy, to so many traitors and spies at the highest circles. But luckily for her, nothing bad happened in her lifetime.

Duke Mislav was informed about Rudolph Mintz and about the plans and drawings of fortresses he'd made for

Venice. Venice was preparing an attack on Hrvatska. When Venice attacked, Hrvatska was prepared and won the battle.

Venice had to sign a peace treaty in 839. Duke Mislav of Hrvatska and Doge Pietro Tradonico of Venice signed the document, which included returning the cities Split, Zadar, and Trogir to Hrvatska. There was also an obligation to pay an annual fee for passage through Hrvatska's part of the Adriatic Sea.

Mislav was a good ruler. The important fact about him was that he defeated his enemy, his enemy hat to sign the peace treaty, and he had good relations with his neighbours. He also made Hrvatska's sea power stronger. He was succeeded by Trpimir.

Trpimir ruled from 845 till 864. That was a period when Christianity was spreading everywhere. It was the period when the duke of Great Moravia asked the Byzantine Church's superior to send teachers to educate his people. They sent two monks, brothers Cyril and Methodius, who translated all church books to the Old Slavic language. Slavs were the first in Europe to have the Church's books and prayers translated into their language. Monks from Cyril and Methodius's school created the Cyrillic alphabet, which is still in use in Bulgaria and Russia, but Hrvatska stuck with Latin.

All further information about Hrvatska was mainly from diaries. When I found the diaries, I did some quick browsing through them. Some of them were obviously missing, and some of them turned to the dust at my touch. Despite that, it was easy to follow the continuity.

That's why this part of the book is titled …

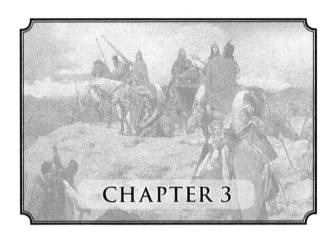

CHAPTER 3

HISTORY

I was shocked after reading just a few diaries. I couldn't believe that that kind of evil existed.

I read the book, I don't remember the title or the writer, but I remember this part very well.

> Long, long ago, people thought that the earth was an even plateau, with good people on the top of it and the monsters under it. Now we know the earth is a globe. Oh, my God! The monsters are among us!"

New Duke of Hrvatska became Trpimir I, founder of the Trpimirovic dynasty. Trpimir (845–864) was the vassal of Frankish Emperor Lothair, but he used conflicts between Byzant and Franks to rule on his own.

He chose Klis, a town in the middle of Dalmatia, to be his capital city, and he built his fortress there.

He had three sons, Peter, Zdeslav, and Muncimir.

CHAPTER 4

YAGODA

All this information was coming from Yagoda's diary. In her diary, she described the events in the time of Domagoy's reign and the events after Domagoy. After Trpimir's death in 864, the ruler of Hrvatska became his son Duke Zdeslav, but he didn't last for long. This Domagoy (the worst duke of Hrvatska) was a nobleman from Knin and raised a rebellion. All three sons of Trpimir I were exiled from Hrvatska to Constantinople.

The diary started with Yagoda's encounter with Emilio Mintz.

Yagoda Nevena's granddaughter, who lived in the Snowy Mountain, decided to go to visit her cousins in Varazdin.[4]

---

[4] Town in Pannonian Hrvatska.

One day on the way home from her fencing training, she had a feeling that somebody was following her.

She discretely dropped the bracelet on the ground, and then she bent as if she was looking for something. She was really watching people behind her. She noticed the man watching her secretly and felt deep animosity. Trying to find the explanation for that feeling, she suddenly realised he looked exactly like Rudolph Mintz. Her all body shouted, *Danger, danger!*

While she was straightening up, he disappeared.

She thought about what to do and concluded that the best thing to do was to talk to Gordan. She went to visit him, checking from time to time if somebody followed her. She was sure that nobody suspicious was around. She reached the house and knocked at the door.

"It's open—come in."

She entered. The house was spacious, built in stone, and comfortable. Two big dogs, German shepherds, jumped off the sofa and ran to meet her. They were beautiful, young dogs that were very playful. They brought their toys. She played with them for a while, and then Gordan shouted, "Mycra, Whisper, enough! Go back to your corner."

They obeyed immediately.

"Hello, dearest cousin. Nice to see you. I was just thinking about you. I like our little chats."

She hugged him and kissed both of his cheeks. "Nice to see you too, but I didn't come just for a chat. I need your help."

"My help? For what? What's happening?"

"I noticed a man watching me secretly. I know that he is my enemy and is up to something. I think he doesn't know you, and so I thought that maybe you could follow him and find out as much as possible about him."

"No problem, I'll do that. Happy to help you. But how will I know the man?"

"Tomorrow, I will have my fencing training again, and I have a feeling that he will be there. I'm sure you will know that man the moment you see him."

Sure enough, the man was there. He was half hidden in one corner, watching with a sardonic smile on his face. After half an hour of her training, he wasn't smiling anymore. Gordan was there as well, looking for him. He saw the face in the corner, and he understood what Yagoda was thinking when she said he would know the man. He also knew the description of Rudolph's face. Following him was easy; the man didn't have any suspicion at all. Gordan found out where the man lived and learned that he lived alone—no friends, no wife, no family. The next day, a smug smile was again on his face.

The man approached her, saying, "Please, lady, don't run away. You don't know me, but I know you. My name is Emilio Mintz, and my intentions are honest. I just want to give you back something that belongs to you. My granddad did bad things to members of your family, and I'm sorry about that. He left me something that belongs to you: this beautiful ring that Prince Node gave to Zoya as a wedding present. I don't know how it ended up in my granddad's hands, but I don't want to keep something that doesn't belong to me. Please take it, put it on your finger, and let it shine on that beautiful hand."

Yagoda took the ring. "Oh, it's magnificent. I can't resist. I'll take it. Thank you very much!"

He was very disappointed when he noticed that she was not going to take off her gloves. The gloves were made from leather, and he knew that the needle couldn't go through it. "It will be much nicer without the gloves," he said.

"I know," said Yagoda, "but I can't take the gloves off. This is a protective suit all in one piece. I guess you would prefer to see it on my finger. Don't worry—you'll be invited on the first occasion when I wear it. Just give your address to my maid."

He was disappointed but couldn't back out. He decided to leave it as it is, hoping that she would try ring the moment she entered her house. "Well," he said, "I did right thing, and I feel much better. Good night."

He waited to see which window would light, and when it happened, he said to himself, *So that's the window through which I'll enter the house.* Satisfied that he now knew where she lived, including her room, he disappeared.

Next morning when Yagoda woke up, she found Fabrizio dead in her room with the ring on his finger. The previous day when she'd come home, she looked very carefully at the ring from all sides and found the needle and the little box with the poison. She carefully turned the needle around so that the needle was pointed out, and when Fabrizio grabbed the ring to get it from her finger the needle pierced his skin, the poison entered in the blood, causing instant death. Yagoda took the ring and hid it. Then she called her host, cousin Michaela, and told her what had happened.

"Michaela, don't be scared, and don't scream." There is a dead body in my room. Don't touch anything I'm just going to bring Gordan and the city pandur."[5]

The pandur examined the body very carefully, and soon he noticed the snake bite on his hand. "This is very strange," he said. "It seems that the snake bit him, but instead of looking for help, he continued with his intention to rob you."

"Snake!" both girls screamed.

"Don't worry, there is no the snake in the house. I think that happened outside, but I will send my two men to search the house to be sure. Let's see if we can find out who this man is." He looked through the intruder's pockets, and in one of them he found the letter addressed to Fabrizio Stoddard, Omisal, Cabana 5. In the letter was just a short message: "I saw one of the girls you're looking for in the same town you're staying at the moment."

He turned toward Gordan. "I'm going to search his house now. Gordan, will you come with me as a witness? You girls had better go for a walk. I will send two men to do a search, and a person from the morgue will take the body. In the meantime, Miss Yagoda, try to remember anything about

---

[5] Policeman.

what this man has against you and what was he looking for in the house."

"Can we go with you? I'm afraid. Maybe he has an accomplice. I never saw this man before, and I don't have any idea what was he looking for."

"OK," said the pandur. Maybe we will find something in his house that will help us resolve this case."

In Emilio's room on the table, they saw lots of drawings of the fortresses.

Yagona shouted, "Traitor! I know now. His granddad was a spy, a traitor. Aunty Vesna sentenced him to be hung."

He knew very well who Aunty Vesna was. For him, the case was closed. Gordan said, "I must check all these papers, sort them out, and then give them to Duke Domagoy to warn him that Venice is preparing a new attack on our country. I know he is nothing like Mislav, but it is my duty to tell him what's happening."

Next morning, he was on the way to Knin, new capital of Hrvatska, chosen by Domagoy.

. Domagoy ruled from 864 to 876. He was too busy to pay attention to this new problem. He was engaged in the inner conflicts about the throne. Apart from that, he was in a war with Byzant; the Byzantine emperor was helping Zdeslav and his brothers back to the throne. Domagoy was in a war with the Arabs attacking Dalmatia's coast, and now this problem with Venice. He really didn't have a time for that.

Venice attacked and defeated him, winning in a big battle in Makarska. Hrvatska again lost the Dalmatian cities Split,

Zadar, and Trogir. Duke Domagoy had to sign a new peace treaty that was very unfavourable for Hrvatska, and apart from that, he had to give hostages as insurance.

In all that turmoil over who would rule, Gordan disappeared.

Yagoda was devastated. She asked everywhere if somebody saw a young man on a black horse heading to Knin, but she couldn't get any information about his whereabouts. She decided to follow his steps. That brought her to Knin. Upon passing through military camp, she noticed one soldier looking at her like he wanted to tell her something but couldn't decide whether to do it.

She stopped, and he said, "Lady, are you Yagoda? If yes, I have a message for you, but first you must guess the name of a messenger."

"Gordan," Yagoda said quickly. "What's the message?"

"We met ten days ago in this camp," said the soldier. "He told me that he doesn't know anybody in Knin, and he needs to leave a message for one person, a girl who will probably come looking for him. He said, 'Please tell her that I've gone to Makarska.'"

She thanked the soldier and decided to continue travelling even though she was very tired. It took her ten days to reach Makarska, only to find out that Gordan was dead. Nobody knew who had killed him.

She was exhausted and frustrated, and she needed rest. The Adriatic Sea looked perfect for that purpose, and she decided to take a cruise.

She sent a messenger to Snowy Mountain with a message for Hope, her younger sister.

> Come to Dalmatia immediately, please. Gordan disappeared. I need you. I'm so tired and frustrated. Maybe one cruise around the Adriatic will calm me down, clear this turmoil in my head, and help me think.

Hope accepted the invitation, and soon they were together and deciding on which yacht to choose. They chose a boat called *Apollo*.

The captain of the boat, Nikola, was coming down to the dock just as Yagoda and Hope came to talk about renting a boat. Hope and Nikola saw each other, and it was love at the first sight. He went down to meet them.

"Hello, my beauties," he said. "Welcome to my boat. I'm the captain and owner of the boat. My name is Nikola."

"Nice to meet you, Nikola," said Hope. "My name is Hope, and this is my sister Yagoda. We were looking around. We would like to go on a cruise. Your boat looks perfect for what we had in mind. It is a lucky coincidence that we met you because my sister is very tired. Would you mind talking business here? Could we rent your boat and your services for a fortnight?"

"I'm afraid you chose a bad time to come. The big battle just finished. Unfortunately, we lost. It's still very dangerous to go out. But I can take you to the Kornati Islands, and you can camp over there in peace and quiet. I will bring you food regularly. You can catch fresh fish if you know anything about fishing."

"No, said Hope, we don't know anything about fishing. But you could stay a few days with us if you're not too busy, to teach us."

"That's a good idea. I must hide my boat from these Venetians anyway," said Nikola. Where are you from?"

"I'm from Snowy Mountain," said Hope. "Tell me what Venetians are doing in our part of the sea."

"They won the battle in Makarska because of the treason. The whole country is full of spies."

"Oh, not again," said Hope.

"I'm afraid so," said Nikola. "But what did you mean by 'Not again'?"

She told him everything about her family, the family oath, the heir discoveries in connection with the spies, and their inability to do more because the duke didn't care.

He told her about how he had uncovered spies on his boat.

"Oh!" interrupted Hope. "They have spies all over our country, and their intention is to get whole coastline from Rijeka to Dubrovnik this time."

"What do you know about that?"

"My sister and I know a lot about it. One of these spies came to Omishal when she was visiting our cousins. He came with the intention to kill her, but she guessed his intention and motives, and he was caught on time. In his rented room, policeman found proof that he is a spy. He had information about every underground passage and secret entrance to all fortresses. He probably got that from his granddad. My family found out all about that, and Duke Mislav had time to prepare a defence and had a great victory.

"But Duke Domagoy is not like Duke Mislav—he doesn't care about Venice and is just fighting for the throne. When we caught this Emilio Mintz, our cousin investigated, uncovered the whole net of spies, and went to visit Duke Domagoy to warn him. Duke Domagoy was already fully engaged in his wars, and Gordan was on his way to visit Domagoy when he disappeared. We think that there are traitors in the highest circles of the government of our country, around our duke. Our pure cousin was killed. As I already said, Duke Domagoy doesn't have time for problems with Venice because he's just fighting for the throne."

CHAPTER 5

NIKOLA

"I have a plan for how to find possible spies between my sailors, and I already started," said Nikola. "You see, Venice's boats are trying to escape paying taxes. They are trying to pass our part of the Adriatic unnoticed, and we always know when they are coming—we have our spies as well. But for the last month, they have managed to escape. My guess is they have informants on our boats, and so I compared the dates when we couldn't find Venetian ships with the dates of new members of the crew. I told all my friends, the other ship owners, to do the same. We have a list of about thirty suspects.

"Now you're telling me that they are in our fortresses. I have an idea about how to catch them, but I don't have an idea about how to catch the traitors in the highest circles. But let's catch those we can. We will give our list to each lord of his fortress, and further action is up to him."

"So what's your idea?" asked Hope.

"While I was working on this problem, it occurred to me that it is not enough to know the entries and passages. They need somebody inside to open the doors, and I think that I have a solution for that. We will sort that out in the places of events."

Nikola quickly called his crew and told them about a possible conspiracy. "Defenders must be worn," said Nikola. He turned toward Hope. "You stay here. We'll talk afterwards."

"I can fight like a man. I'm going with you," said Hope.

"I knew that we are one soul in two bodies. Let's skip all formalities and get married. We have no time to lose. We will have our honeymoon after the war."

"Can we leave Yagoda in your brother's house? I wouldn't like to leave her alone."

"Sure, we can," said Nikola.

Nikola was talking a lot about Hope's family oaths. He couldn't forget that thanks to that, and the heroism and patriotism of Hrvatska's warriors, they had defeated Venice in the time of Maslar's reign.

He said, "Oaths are noble. I want to be in that battle with you. But first things first. We must find out who the traitors are. We should go to Dubrovnik, as well, to visit my old friend Samuel. He is a goldsmith. We will ask him to rearrange the ring."

"That's very good idea," Hope said.

They went together to Dubrovnik. Nikola's friend was very glad to see them. He said, "The simplest change is to change the mechanism that activates the needle—the way that the needle reacts to push and pricks the person who did the pushing. Just be very careful while you are handling it."

"OK," said Nikola. "We will leave the ring with you, and we're going to continue with our plans. As for the ring, don't you upset yourself. We will be careful."

In their visit to Split, Zadar, and Trogir, the investigators found out that every fortress had three men who could operate inside the secret door. Nikola rampaged through their rooms in their absence, and in one of them he found what was he looking for: the letter from Prince. Now that he had the type of paper and a sample of Prince's writing, he made copies. He wrote messages asking each of them to leave the secret entry unlocked, each of them at a different time. Then he put the messages in places he thought suitable for hiding secret messages.

He got his culprits without much ado. He called their lords and explained them the situation: how he'd prepared the trap for them, checked the door every time, and found them unlocked just once under the care of one certain person. He knew that person was the traitor. They were accused, found guilty, and executed.

When he finished that task, Hope said, "Nikola, I want to go home. I need some rest because I'm pregnant."

He jumped excitedly and started hugging and kissing her. "Oh, my love, my dear Hope. And I sent you into danger! Why didn't you say something?"

"Nikola, I'm pregnant. That happens to women, you know. I'm pregnant, not sick, you, silly bear."

At that moment, one of his sailors showed up at the door. "Hi, Captain. Hi, Mrs Hope. Hi, everybody! Captain, I must talk to you."

"You can say whatever you need to in front of Hope. Tell me. We are all trusted here."

"I went yesterday to visit the city judge," said the sailor. "I asked him if he needed our help in anything, because we were going soon home, and we didn't want to leave anything unsolved. His housekeeper told me that he was in the court, and so I went over there. He was talking to one of our sailors, and he didn't see me.

"'Be patient, Dario. They will soon take off. There's just one little problem: Lady Hope is pregnant. They are waiting for the weather to settle down.'"

"'Pregnant! We must inform Marta about that.'

"'Don't worry—that's already taken care of.'"

"Oh! The situation is much worse than I thought," said Nikola. He turned towards Hope. "We can't do anything here. Let's go home."

Domagoy died the next year and was succeeded by his son. But Zdeslav, with help from Byzantine Emperor Basil I, overthrew him in 878. He was expelled from the country. Zdeslav overtook his throne and power again. Zdeslav made peace with Venice and acknowledged the supreme rule of Byzant. The next year, Zdeslav was killed.

The new duke became Branimir, Domagoy's relative.

Very disappointed with what was happening, Hope and Nikola went home to their lovely Makarska. After a few more months, they had twins, two sons. They named them Jakob and Miroslav. Jakob was nothing like his parents—very skinny, pale, and sickly looking. Hope was very disappointed. Miroslav, on the other hand, was a beautiful boy—healthy, good-natured, and a funny little face.

The midwife came every day to help Hope and tried to comfort her, telling her that Jakob would change through the coming years; he would likely grow into a big, strong man just like Nikola. She would say, "This is temporary. That boy is very healthy."

But Hope didn't believe that. Her heart was cold, and she couldn't warm up to the child. The child cried all the time, and she felt guilty, thinking that reason for that was her coldness. Everybody loved Miroslav. Jakob was very jealous, and he spent most of his time with the midwife, Marta. Marta took good care of Jakob. Everybody thought that she felt sorry for the boy.

Hope was very tired with all the work in the house and keeping track of two boys. She didn't have time to follow and destroy evil. One day, she decided to talk about that to Nikola. But first she must to talk to her sons. She took them for a walk. When they reached her favourite place, Tutchepi, she said, "Let's sit here on the pebbles and enjoy this sunny day. Listen to the murmur of the sea and let this beauty and calmness fill your soul."

They were looking at her with wide eyes. They were so young, at eight years. She wondered whether they were old enough to understand what she was talking about,

"I want you to know that I and your father love you more than anything and anybody in the world. We love you both the same, and if you, Jakob, think that we love Miroslav more you're wrong. It's just that Miroslav is easier to go on. Dear child, don't let the green monster grow in your heart."

"Maybe you and Daddy love me the same, even if it doesn't look like it. But nobody else does. And what is the green monster, Mammy?"

"Envy, my dear child. It poisons the heart and destroys the soul. "Furthermore, you can't say that only I and your dad love you. Your brother loves you; and what about Marta? It seems to me that she loves you most of all."

"I love my brother," said Jakob, "and I don't like Marta."

"You see, Jakob?" said Hope. "There are two type of people. There are people who like to make other people happy, and there are people who are happy when everybody around them is unhappy, and they will do anything to make them unhappy."

Poor mammy, thought one. *I should try to make her happy. What a full,* thought the other one.

"And the dogs love him the most," said Miroslav. "They are following him everywhere." The dogs were Mycra and

Whisper, Gordan's dogs. Yagoda took care of them after Gordan's disappearance.

That evening, Hope said to Nikola, "I had little chat today with the boys. It seems to me that Marta has a bad influence on Jakob. I'm not going to let her destroy my children's soul."

Nikola said, "I agree. Do you have any idea how to solve this?"

"I was thinking about your brother Marko. He is very good young man, and he loves our children. The children adore him. I thought we could tell him about our duties, the documentation and proof of Venetian plots we collected and gave to Domagoy, and how he, in his greed and thirst for power, destroyed already achieved victories. Tell him that we must go to visit Duke Muncimir, inform him about everything that's already done, investigate the current situation, and finish with the spies, traitors, and plotters. Ask him if he could take care of the children, Yagoda, and the dogs. The dogs are trained guard dogs."

"Good thinking," said Nikola. "Let's do it now."

Marko was very surprised to see them so late. "What's up, people? Where is the fire?"

"Eh, Marko," said Nikola, "you're always ready for a laugh. We came to talk about a serious and urgent matter."

"shoot! I'm all ears."

Nikola told him the whole story. Marko sat there and listened with an open mouth. "What adventure," he said. "I would rather go with you."

"Don't you worry," said Hope. "You will have your own time. When we decide to retire, we will transfer duties on to you."

"Of course," said Marko. "I'll do everything to help you."

"Well, that's done. Tomorrow we'll bring Yagoda, the kids, and the dogs. Please do all this secretly. We don't want Marta to know anything about this. Then we're going to visit Duke Muncimir."

Muncimir was Zdeslav's younger brother. He reigned from Bianchi near Trogir and ruled from 892 to 910. He ruled independently. During the time of his rule, Hungarians showed up in that part of Europe. They invaded Northern Italy.

After Muncimir's death, Hrvatska's ruler became Tomislav, the first king of Hrvatska. Tomislav started as Duke of Hrvatska in 910 and became king in 925. He ruled as king till 928.

Hrvatska had rows everywhere along the border, but King Tomislav managed to keep the borders, and he even expanded his country to part of the disintegrated Pannonia Duchy.

Tomislav was celebrated as the first king of Hrvatska the and founder of the first united Hrvatska country.

Hope and Nikola finished their chores, informed the king about ruthless enemies all around his borders, and returned home. They'd done a great job, but still they were restless, feeling that something important was missing.

One day Nikola was looking for Hope and found her in the garden. Hope was sitting on the garden bench, lost in thought.

"There you are," said Nikola. "Let's go for a little cruise: Dubrovnik, Peljeshac (the peninsula in the south of Adriatic), Locrum, Lastovo, and the Vis Islands. It will clear up our heads. What do you say?"

"Good idea," said Hope. "Lt's go."

They packed the necessities and headed out.

The second day of their tour, the weather changed. A wind called bura[6] got stronger and stronger. Nikola heard a strange noise like wood cracking, and he looked up and noticed that the mainmast was intentionally damaged. He called Hope.

"Come here, my darling. Hug me. We're going to die today. Somebody damaged mainmast. What was I doing? Where were my eyes?"

She talked to herself. "The eyes, his eyes. Oh, stupid me."

At that moment, the mainmast broke and fell. The big waves turned the yacht over. The sea covered everything.

That night, Yagoda woke up in the middle of the night with a scream. "They are dead, Marko! They are dead! The sea took them. What's happening? Who are our hidden enemies? Who killed my Gordan? Who killed my sister and your brother?"

---

[6] The wind from the north.

Time passed—days weeks, a month—without any news about Hope and Nikola. In the end, they had to accept the horrible truth: Hope and Nikola were dead.

"That was to be expected," said Marko. "When Nevena swore her family would protect innocence and fight for justice, they all knew that was a very dangerous path."

CHAPTER 6

MARKO

Marko knew that that dangerous duty was his responsibility from that moment. Hope visited him before going on the cruise to say bye to the children and to let them know where they were going. She chose that opportunity to transfer all oaths to Marko.

Marko took that job very seriously, and the citizens of Makarska elected him for city judge.

One evening while he was walking along a dark street, he noticed one old woman pulling a young girl by the arm, forcing her to go with her. The girl was crying, "Let me go! I don't want to go with you. I'm a good girl!"

"Where are you taking this girl?" Marko asked the old woman. Then he asked the girl, "Is this woman your relative?"

"She is nothing to me. She wants me to be a prostitute!"

Marko was very angry, and he said to the woman, "I'm taking this girl with me. Get lost."

He brought the girl to his house and called his housekeeper. "Maria, this girl will be with us. Take good care of her and give her some housework to do." The boys were looking at the girl with admiration. She was a real beauty. They were both enchanted.

When they all went to sleep, Miroslav couldn't sleep. He was thinking about the girl all the time. But he was very worried about Yagoda. He didn't see Yagoda and the dogs all day long. *Is it possible that she …? That's impossible.*

Finally, he got up and entered Marko's room. "Uncle, are you asleep?"

"No, what's up?"

"Uncle, I like that girl very much. I'd like to marry her. I can't sleep. I must know now what she feels."

"Is that really so urgent?" OK, call Maria."

Maria came immediately, like she was expecting something it.

"Maria, see if … I didn't even ask her for her name."

"Her name is Renata," said Maria.

"See if she is awake. If she is, ask her nicely to come into the sitting room for a little chat. This boy has a question for her."

"Oh, I know the question, and I think I know the answer to that."

When Maria left the room, Miroslav said, "Uncle, where is Yagoda? I didn't see her or the dogs all day long."

"Oh, Yagoda is OK. She has gone with the man she loves."

"But—"

"Don't ask me anything. I don't want to talk about it," said Marko.

Soon Renata joined them. Marko said to her, "My dear child, do you have parents or any relatives?"

"No," she said. I'm an orphan. They found me seventeen years ago in a church in Bashka Voda."

"So you are seventeen years old?"

"Yes."

"OK, Miroslav, ask your question."

Miroslav fell on his knees. "Sweet Renata, will you marry me?"

"Yes," she said shyly with tears running down her face.

Nobody slept in that house that night. They were making plans for the wedding and the honeymoon, as well as what they would do and where they'd live when they came back from the honeymoon.

Marko had a nice piece of land at a beautiful location, and he gave them as a wedding present to build a house on it. Miroslav was a blacksmith, and their future was provided.

The wedding was held in the same church where Renata was left as a baby.

Marko continued to secretly follow the old woman. He noticed her entering one isolated house. He called the city's pandur to come with him, and they forcibly entered the house while the old woman was away. In the house, they found sixteen girls tied to beds. They released them and waited for the old woman's return. When she saw them, she tried to escape, but the pandur were fast. They put her in the jail, but the next day they found her dead in her cell.

Marko decided to retire, and he transferred his blacksmith's job to Miroslav. He transferred the family duties he'd accepted from Nikola and Hope to Jakob.

Marko had his doubts, and over time they became stronger. Finally, he decided to try to find the boat. First he had to do some calculations. A good part of the calculations was based on guesses, but he was sure he'd make it.

1. Place and time of start—fact
2. Direction of movement and destination—guess
3. Time when the wind started—fact
4. Direction and the strength of the wind—fact
5. Sinking (time of Yagoda's scream)—fact
6. The time passed (difference between 1 and 5)

When he did his calculation, the result was the coast of the island Vis, between the islands Rukavac and Milna.

He found a boat in shallow water closer to Milna, and so he didn't even have to dive. The diary was in a waterproof box. The last words were, "Those eyes, those cold, hypnotising snake eyes. My God—they are not our children. They killed us."

I reached for Jakob's diary, but when I touched it, it turned to the dust. The same happened with some other diaries. When I continued browsing through them, one tiny diary fell out. On the first page was written "Renata". Somebody had hidden it in the bigger diary. I opened it and started reading.

CHAPTER 7

RENATA

Old witch Agatha didn't let me go. She was telling me how good a life I would have if I accepted her offer. The man who wanted me was very rich, and he would take good care of me.

Her main argument was as follows.

What is good in serving other people, cleaning their houses, cooking their meals, looking after their crying babies? I would just look older than I really was, and I would soon lose my beauty.

I didn't want to listen to her, but she was persistent.

One raining evening when nobody was on the streets and I was going home after a hard day's work, she showed up, grabbed my arm, and started pulling me.

That lovely man, a city judge, suddenly showed up and stopped her. I liked that man. He brought me into his house.

What a horror: right there at the kitchen table sat the person who was the cause of all my troubles—the young man who wanted me to be his mistress.

I was speechless, but I managed to look like I'd never seen him in my life. I noticed that he was tense when I entered the sitting room and that he relaxed when I didn't react to his appearance.

The same night, he proposed. Oh, Marko! Why didn't you do that? I knew that you liked me. I saw the pain in your eyes when Miroslav proposed. I knew that I must accept or we would all die that night. Yes, it was Miroslav, the cruel criminal. Marta took Hope's babies. By coincidence, her cousin was pregnant at the same time as Hope, and she swapped the babies. She took them very often to her house, and there she poisoned their little souls, talking against their parents. Jakob didn't like that. He loved his mother, but Miroslav was his God.

I had a duty to help old people who lived in the villages close to our town with their daily chores. I brought them meals for the day and helped them dress. I would usually do some essential cleaning so I could be around Miroslav as little as possible. He soon lost interest in me and was often away for days, which suited me perfectly. But old women were the biggest gossipers. It became a routine: small talk about health, about weather, and then everybody's business but theirs.

One day, one of them said, "My dear woman, you are so lucky that you don't have children. The young and beautiful girls are disappearing. Those poor mothers."

I knew what was happening. I knew I had to talk to Marko. I found him in the kitchen talking to Marta about something, but he stopped when I entered.

I said, "Marko, I must talk to you. I need to talk with both of you. Please, Maria, don't go—stay and listen." I told them everything.

He asked me, "Why didn't you tell me immediately? I've had my doubts for a while now but didn't do anything because I thought you loved him."

"No, I love you," I said.

"Why didn't you tell me before? Oh, dear God, so much time lost!"

That came out like a scream, and after that, he left the room. A few minutes after he went out of the room, Maria said, "Renata, dear child, why didn't you tell us sooner? He is now in his room crying like a child."

At that moment, he entered the sitting room again. "Miroslav is here," he said.

Miroslav entered the room with Jakob, but Jakob took a glass of water and went out.

"Oh, look at my conspirators, all together. My dear wife. All the love and goodness. My caring uncle, the law, which doesn't have any proof for my crimes. He is powerless because he must respect the law."

Marko put a hand in his jacket pocket to get a tissue, but instead of tissue he brought out a beautiful ring. "Oh, I forgot to put this back. I'm just going to do that now. You wait here—I must talk to you," said Marko.

Miroslav stopped him. "You're not going anywhere. That's my mother's ring. Give it to me, Mr Thieving."

Then he jumped and grabbed the ring. He felt the sharp pain, and the last thing that he heard were Marko's words.

"I'm not the law—I'm justice!"

Death from a snake's bait was the official conclusion.

Marko had a long conversation with Jakob, trying to find out whether Jakob was in the crime business with Miroslav.

"No. I hate violence and crime of any kind. I just didn't do anything to stop him. I was afraid of him."

One year after Miroslav's death, Renata and Marko got married. A year later, they had twins, a girl named Yadranka and a boy named Gordan. They were new warriors for justice and independence. Hrvatska really needed them.

Six days after the twins' birth, Marta's daughter, Marta Younger, showed up at the door. "Why didn't you call me? You know that I, as a midwife, must take care of newborn children."

"We are OK," said Marko. "We have Maria, who is a midwife too."

Two days after that visit, we found Maria dead in her bed with a look of horror on her face.

Jacob disappeared. That night, Marko was absent.

He woke me up early in the morning and said, "Pack only the most necessary things. We're leaving. Don't let anybody see you packing."

Around midnight, Marko took our horse. He wrapped up the horse's legs with towels and put everything on the horse, with the babies well protected. Our escape started. We didn't exit the house, but we went to the basement, where Marko uncovered a hidden entry into a tunnel made a long ago for escape in a case of enemy attack. The tunnel was made like a maze, and only Marko knew how to find the exit. The tunnel was very long, and the exit was in the Biokovo Mountain. We spent two weeks in that maze, and suddenly a dog showed up.

"Don't be afraid," said Marko. "That's our dog. Her name is Tara. We can continue our trip; our passage is free now."

"What do you mean, free now? Wasn't it free before? And where did that dog come from? You are suddenly full of secrets," I said.

"Calm down, sweetheart. I will explain it to you. Remember the story about Nevena coming home after Mintz's attack? She was escorted by a wolf."

"Yes," I said. "I remember very well. I was so jealous that I didn't have the same kind of friend."

"That was Nevena's wolf—a wolverine, in fact. She found her in the woods alone, frostbitten, and hungry. She warmed her up by hugging and petting her. At first she fed her with milk, and after a few weeks, when the dog was stronger, she fed it meat. She wanted her to keep all her animal and instincts. Then she crossed her with a German shepherd. Every generation she continued to mix the wolf with the dog. She left instructions to her family to continue doing so, but not for the public—just for the close family. When Mycra had puppies, I kept one female and crossed it with a wild wolf.

Please don't ask me how I did it; it was very hard. I succeeded on my third try."

"But how did you manage to keep that a secret all these years?" asked Renata.

"Oh, that was the least of my problems. I have one very good friend in the nearby village, Srebreno. We are like brothers—more than brothers, really. You get a brother by birth, but you choose a pobratim.[7] I saved his and his family's lives during the Venetian attack on Makara.

"After their parents disappeared, the boys behaved very strangely. I caught Jakob looking at Yagoda with hate, and his eyes became smaller as he concentrated on her, like he was trying to hypnotise her. It was like a snake's eyes. I told her that, and she said that she noticed it and would like to go home to the Snowy Mountains. I agreed with her, and a few days later when the boys were away, I brought her to my pobratim's house, where she stayed a week until we found safe transport for her. But as I said, we can continue our trip now. The air is clean."

"What do you mean?"

"Jakob was after us. He is like a dog, and so I left my dog to take care of that, which he did."

"Where are we going?"

To Zagreb. By the way, do you know the legend of how Zagreb got its name?"

"No, I don't. Please tell me. I love legends."

7

"It was long ago in the time of the crusades, in the place where Zagreb is today. It was at the well. Beside the well was a girl, Manda, from the nearby village. She was taking water.

"A tired, thirsty warrior came to the well and said, 'Good morning, girl. What's your name?'

"'My name is Manda,' she said, 'but everybody calls me Mandusa.'

"He gave her his bottle and said, 'Zagrabi (scoop), Mandusa, and from that zagrabi became Zagreb.'"

"Nice story," said Renata.

We continued our travels from mountain to mountain—(Biokovo, Dinara, Velebit, and Gorski Kotar—with short stops to take a break and catch some food. Marko was a very good hunter.

When we reached Zagreb, we bought a lovely house, changed names, and started a new, quiet life.

CHAPTER 8

STANKO

Stanko started his duty at the same time Tomislav took the throne.

Tomislav was the first king of Hrvatska. He repelled the attack of Hungarians who began crossing the Drava River and reached the Adriatic. He became an ally with Byzant during the Bulgarian expansion, and the Byzant emperor allowed him to rule over Dalmatia.

Pope John X, in a letter, called Tomislav king of Hrvatska.

Bulgarian Tsar Simeon attacked Hrvatska with strong forces led by Duke Alogobotur, and King Tomislav defeated him.

CHAPTER 9

MARKO: SECOND DIARY

In Zagreb, we joined a group that called themselves the Association for Preservation of National Identity.

One morning, Marko came home very excited and worried. He was going to the market to buy few things for the local library when he heard a familiar voice.

He looked over his shoulder. It was Marta with her daughter and granddaughter. She was saying, "Don't worry. I would have recognised him anywhere. He can't hide from me. "Please, Renata, don't go away from the house. Don't open the door for anyone for the time being. I will send the messenger to my pobratim[8] Ivek to ask him to do whatever is needed to get rid of these horrible women."

---

[8] Brother's bood.

Ivek took care of everything. He entered Marta's house and her found books in one of the hidden drawers. One of the books consisted of the evidence of all born and exchanged children. The other one was a list of all customers to whom she'd sold poisons or love pots. The latter he brought straight to the magistrate and accused Marta and her family of using magic powers and poisoning people. Regarding the books about exchanged children, he kept it and gave it to Marko. The proof was very hard, and Marta and family didn't have a chance to escape execution. During the night, somebody put the jail on fire, and Marta and her family, and all her books, burned. Only Marta Youngest managed to escape that destiny; she wasn't home when her mother and her grandma were arrested.

Ivek didn't bring the books about exchanged children to the magistrate because it would be very hard on families to know that their children were not really their own. That knowledge could bring a lot of trouble to families. He gave that book to Marko. Through the complete procedure and after gathering the evidence, Marko's name wasn't mention anywhere.

When Marko got the book, his first errand was to find his brother's children. From the book he learned that they were given to the family Golovec in the village of Yazovka. He went to Yazovka immediately.

When he got there, he entered a local shop to find out something about the family Golovec. He was lucky because the owner of the shop and his ancestors had lived in that village for two centuries now, and he knew everybody and everything about local people. His name was Mladen.

"And you're coming all the way from Zagreb to ask me about the Golovecs?" said Mladen. "I will tell you this. You're maybe from that family. You look honest, man, and I want you to meet yourself."

"What do you mean by that? Meet myself?" asked Marko.

"Wait and see," answered Mladen.

After these words, Mladen locked the shop and told Marko to come with him. They walked through the village without a word. Mladen stopped in front of one nice white house and called out, ""Marinko, are you home? Come out, I have a surprise for you."

Marinko came out, saying, "Is something wrong, Uncle? You're early today." He stopped with his mouth wide open. Marko couldn't believe his own eyes. Tears blurred his eyes. In front of him stood his own image.

Mladen interrupted this silence. "Let's go in the house. Let's hear your story, mister."

They entered the house and sat around the table. Mladen brought a bottle of wine, some cheese, and proshut[9] with bread. In that comfortable atmosphere, Marko told them the whole story.

"Can I hear your story now?" he asked.

"Of course," said Mladen. "Golovec Brundaš and his wife, Fiona, were our neighbours. Evil people—always drunk,

---

[9] Smoked pork meat.

always arguing and fighting. When she became pregnant, we hoped they would calm down. Wishful thinking. They became even worse. Poor little kids were badly fed and worse treated. We couldn't listen anymore to that screaming and the children crying. One day when they were gone out, I went to their house, took the children, and brought them into my house. My wife fed them, and they fell asleep. I thought I would let them sleep for a while in the peace and quiet and then bring them to their house, but Brundash and Fiona came back sooner than I'd expected. Believe it or not, they never asked where their children were and what had happened to them."

In that moment, another young man came to the house.

"And this is my other stepson, Dario. I couldn't be happier if they were my own flesh and blood. You chose the right moment to come. If you had come a few days later, you wouldn't find us. I inherited big property in Ponte, a nice little town on the island of Krk, and we are moving. After we get settled, we will come to Zagreb to visit you. You were lucky to find us, and we will keep constant contact."

Marko said that he would be glad to keep contact with all family. He was lost in thought all the way to Zagreb. He had one idea. He was more and more certain that Mintz's family had a widespread net to hunt down Nevena's descendants. He realised that he must make a plan for defence. His enemy was ruthless, and they were not just after Yagelovichs—they were after Hrvatska, and they are going to destroy Hrvatska's every attempt to win independence.

He already had three starting points.

- This association in Zagreb that he'd joined; they should cover Zagreb and Slavonia
- His pobratim Ivek, for Dalmatia
- Family in Punat, for Rijeka and Hrvatska's Primorje.

He made the plan, including all his friends whom he knew very well. He was sure that he could count on them. He invited them to his house and explained what had started that vendetta and what type of people they were against. They all accepted his plan.

Marko was a man of action, and he left good people to continue with his job.

Here was missing, probably, a diary or two.

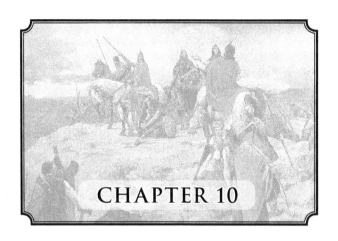

CHAPTER 10

VENZEL (TRPIMIR II—ZVONIMIR)

According to Venzel's diary, during the reigns of Trpimir II and Kresimir I, Hrvatska managed to keep good relations with Byzant and the pope. But during Miroslav's and Kresimir II's reigns, the inner conflicts around the throne started again, and Pannonian Ban killed Miroslav. That weakened Hrvatska. But King Kresimir managed to restore Hrvatska's power, and Byzant managed to re-establish its power over the Dalmatian cities and islands.

When King Krešimir died, the new king was Stephen Držislav, who had good relations with Byzant. Byzant returned him Dalmatian cities and islands. After his death, inner conflicts over the crown started again between his sons, Svetoslav, Krešimir, and Gojslav. Venice used that opportunity to attack Hrvatska again from one side, and Macedonian

Samuilo attacked from the other side. He penetrated to Zadar and from there unsuccessfully attacked Byzant's towns in the southern part. In 1000 BC, Venetian Dode Petar Orsolo II, with quick naval action, won over the whole of Dalmatia from Krk to Dubrovnik.

Hrvatska's kings throughout the eleventh century tried to win back Dalmatia. King Kresimir succeeded in winning over some cities on the north, but in 1018 Venice took them back.

Kresimir's son, Stephen I, continued to strengthen the country. Small parishes became larger territorial and administrative areas.

The country was divided into twelve zupa,[10] which were ruled by zupan.[11]

After Stephen's death, the new king was Petar Kresimir IV. During his reign, Hrvatska was the strongest and the biggest.

The next king was Dmitar Zvonimir.

---

[10] County.
[11] Prefect.

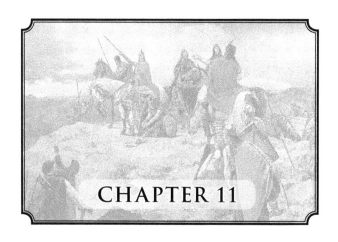

CHAPTER 11

DAREN

Zvonimir was king of Hrvatska and Dalmatia from 1075 until his death in 1089. He was crowned in Solin on 8 October 1076 with the St Stephen crown received from the pope. His capital city was Knin. Hrvatska was very strong during his rule, but he made two big mistakes:

The first was a military obligation to the pope, which caused his death. He was killed because nobility didn't want to go in a faraway country like Jerusalem to fight over Jesus's grave. They were plotting against King Zvonimir and were complaining between themselves about how they couldn't get killed overseas. They were offering a big sum of money.

Daren was sitting with friends in the local inn. He heard that complaining, and he couldn't believe the man from his table murmured loudly enough, "Obviously not big enough."

"Be quiet," said Daren. "They don't need you to give them ideas."

"Ouch," said the man. "I didn't know that I said that aloud."

"Next time, first think and then talk, because as our people say, words are not dogs—once let out, they can't be called back."

The next day, King Zvonimir was killed. Daren tried to find the man but without success.

Legend said that the dying king caused Hrvats to not have independence for nine hundred years.

Zvonimir's second mistake was that he married the sister of the Hungarian king, the beautiful Helena.

After Zvonimir's death, Helena gave Hrvatska's crown to her brother, Arpad, and with the crown went Hrvatska as well.

Nobility chose a new king, Petar Snacic. But Hungary came with big forces and defeated Hrvatska's army in the battle on Gvozd Mountain.

CHAPTER 12

BASED ON ADRIAN'S DIARY

The kingdom of Hrvatska entered into a personal union with Hungary in 1102, after the death of King Petar Snacic. That meant Hrvatska kept all its rights, laws, and habits. The ruler of Hrvatska was now Ban. Ban was chosen by the king, and he was responsible for the judiciary, finances, and (in the case of war) forming an army and helping the king of Hungary. All that was put on the paper Pacta Conventa but never signed.

Hrvatska was now divided into ten zupa with Zupan on top. Zupan was a member of Sabor.[12]

In 1102, Hrvatska was again separated in two parts, Pannonia and Dalmatia.

---

[12] Senate.

Dalmatia was under the rule of Venice, which lasted for about four hundred years. Hrvats in Dalmatia often had conflicts with Venice for their freedom. They temporarily freed some big city or island, but Venice won it back every time. Venice was in constant conflict with pirates. Pirates from Omis were the most powerful and fearsome in the Mediterranean Sea. They had a special type of boat with a very shallow draught that enabled them to hide in places with very shallow waters, where other ships couldn't pass. They called these boats the arrows, and they were very fast in their attack and escape. In 1444, Venice attacked with a big naval force and defeated Omis, and that was the end of them.

In 1797, Venice became part of the Habsburg Monarchy, and 1866 via voting it became part of Italy.

CHAPTER 13

BASED ON ROBERT'S DIARY

The next king of Croatia was Coloman. He ruled from 1097 till 1116. Coloman and his brother Almos were too young to take the throne; their uncle ascended to the throne. The uncle named his younger nephew Almos as his heir because Coloman was half blind and humpbacked. Coloman escaped from Hungary, but when his uncle died, he came back and managed to ascend to the throne. His brother tried to dethrone him several times, and in retaliation Coloman blinded him and his son, Bela.

The next ruler of Hrvatska was Stephen II, Coloman's son. He ruled from 1116 to 1131. His father crowned him when he was four years old to prevent his brother Almos from taking the throne. In the first year of his rule, Venice occupied Dalmatia, and Stephen never managed to win it back.

Doge Ordelafo Falleero came back with a Venetian fleet and defeated Stephen II, who tried to rule over the coastline of the Adriatic Sea. Venice won over the cities Biograd, Sibenik, Split, and Trogir. Then Stephen II attacked again and won, but the new doge, Domenico Michele, reconquered all of Dalmatia again.

He tried to conquer a few more countries but without success.

After his death, the new ruler was Bela II the Blind.

CHAPTER 14

ACCORDING TO ANTUN'S DIARY

The next ruler of Hrvatska was Bella II the Blind, who ruled from 1131 to 1141). He was blinded by Coloman, his uncle. Under his reign, Hungary adopted an active foreign policy. Bosnia and Split (Hrvatska's town on the Adriatic coast) accepted his sovereignty.

All in all, there wasn't a lot happening in Hrvatska during this period. It seemed that nobles were satisfied with Hungarian rule. Bosnia accepted Hungarian sovereignty as well.

Geza II (1141–1162) was the son of Bela II the Blind and Jelena Urošević. He was too young to ascend the throne, and his mother and her brother, Belos, ruled instead of him. In June 1147, German crusaders passed through Hungary. Two months later, Louis VII of France came with his crusaders together with Boris Kalamanos, who used that opportunity to come back to Hungary. When Geza asked Louis VII to extradite him, Louis VII refused to do that but took him to Constantinople. They knew to behave, but they wanted a bit of excitement.

The next king of Hrvatska was Stephen III (1162–1172), the son of Geza II. His two uncles challenged his claim to the throne. They had the support of Byzantine Emperor Manuel I Komnenos. He forced Hungarian nobles to accept Ladislaus for the king. A year later, Vladislaus died, and his brother Stephen IV ascended throne.

Antun was sitting at the table in the kitchen and thinking about the past. The ghosts of the past were everywhere. He was thinking about his ancestor Marko, and how Marko had made plans which save them for two centuries now.

After meeting his nephews, Marko was sure that in Hrvatska there existed an organised group of people, in both Hrvatskas Banovina (Pannonian) and Dalmatian, who want to destroy the Yagelović family and their friends.

When he came back to Zagreb, he started to make plans. He usually sat at the kitchen table, enjoying the noises of his children and Renata's talk. He wrote in one big notebook everything that they were talking about, knowing that would help him to get ideas about their survival. He didn't have any intention of letting fate decide what would happen to his family and friends. When he thought that he had all he needed on paper, he invited them to visit him. That was a warm-hearted meeting.

He started the story in the way it happened, with rape and punishment. Then he said, "There are lot of events I could explain, such as revenge, because it's impossible to have so many accidents in one family. Please, all of you, be very careful.

"First, change your names and family history. Second, don't tell anybody about that change—ever. Between so many towns, choose one to support your life story, but before you start talking about it, go to that town, familiarise yourself with it, meet some eminent people from that town, become friends, and then organise the new lives for yourself and your family. Don't talk too much. Be very nice to your neighbours and help whenever is needed.

Third and the most important, in your stories stick as much as possible to the truth. Stay connected but always in the public places. In a pub, a glass of wine is the best camouflage."

When they finished, they burned the book, but they lived and behaved by the book. Antun also lived by that book. Antun had a very sympathetic neighbour whom he often met in the local pub. Antun used these opportunities to present himself as a person who liked a glass or two over the limit. At the same time, he was able to find out a lot about his neighbourhood and the area.

This neighbour, Martin, would usually start with, "My dear man, you are so secretive. People are asking me all the time about you, such as where are you from, why you insist on talking just in Hrvatska's language, and where you met this gorgeous woman that is your wife. But I have nothing to tell them."

What do they want to know?" asked Antun. "I'm just an ordinary man."

"You can trust me," said Martin. "I'm not going to tell anybody."

"That's OK," said Antun. "I know that you won't tell anybody—especially because I'm not going to tell you, or anybody else, anything. My life is my own business."

On another occasion, the neighbour said, "Antun, you always call your wife, and when you are talking about your wife, you always say 'my princess'. Is she an actual princess?"

"Yes," Antun said. "She is and always will be my princess."

Finally, the neighbour gave up. Antun was a very good neighbour, always ready to help with money and work. He said to the man who asked him questions, "Man, go and ask him yourself."

Then he came to Antun and said, "I don't know what this man from Makarska has against you, but he's plotting all the time. You must be very careful. He looks like a dangerous man, like a criminal, and he is always surrounded with a group of people who look dangerous. I have a feeling that they wouldn't hesitate to kill."

"I honestly don't know them, but thank you for telling me that. I think he's more interested in my wife than me, but for some reason I don't think that's because of her looks. She's a real beauty, isn't she? But I'm going to hire a private investigator to find out what he is up to."

This happened during the time of King Emeric (1196–1204). He cooperated with the Holy See against Bosnian Patarens. The Catholic Church thought that they were heretics.

When he was on his death bed, he crowned his son even though he was just four years old. But he was too young, and the dying king named his brother, Duke Andrew, to be regent while Ladislaus was young. He didn't intend to give the throne to Ladislaus. Ladislaus's mother fled to Austria and brought the child to Vienna, where the child unexpectedly died.

Andrew ascended the throne in 1205 and ruled until 1235.

Here, two or three diaries are missing, or nobody wanted to write them because there wasn't anything to write about Pannonian Hrvatska. The nobles were OK with Hungarian kings ruling, and they had everything like in the time of Byzantine ruling. If they needed military help, the Hungarian king prepared military forces for them.

Bela III reigned from 1235 to 1270. Then Stephen V ascended the throne from 1270 to 1272. He was the oldest son of Hungarian King Bela IV. His father crowned him at the age of seven, naming him the Ban of Hrvatska, Dalmatia, and Slavonia. While he was still a child, his father married him to Elisabeth, a daughter of Cuman's leader. In 1241 Mongols passed over frozen River Danube to Hungary. King Bela escaped to Zagreb with his whole family, but the Mongols reached Zagreb, destroying everything along their way. Bela and family escaped as far as the Dalmatian city Trogir. The Mongols suddenly stopped and went back because their chieftain died.

Stephen V wasn't a good ruler. He fought with the other members of his family over the countries he was given to rule. He died in 1272.

The next king of Hungary and Hrvatska was King Ladislaus IV the Cuman (1272–1290). He was the son of Stephen V and Elisabeth, daughter of the Cuman chieftain. When he was seven years old, his father married him to Elisabeth, daughter of King Charles of Sicily. When he was ten, Lord Joaschim Gutkeled kidnapped and imprisoned him. He was still in prison when his father died. Because of that, lots of aspirants for throne started fighting for supreme power. Even when Ladislaus was freed, he couldn't restore royal power in Hungary.

A papal legate, Philip, came to help, but he was shocked when he saw a thousand pagan Cumans all over the country. Ladislaus promised that he would force them to become Christians, but they preferred to leave Hungary.

Cuman's army attacked Hungary in 1282, but Ladislaus defeated them.

Mongols attacked him twice, but the barons accused him of inciting these attacks.

CHAPTER 15

ACCORDING TO RATIMIR'S DIARY

In 1286m Ladislaus imprisoned his wife, took all her revenue, and gave them to his mistress, a Cuman girl. He preferred the Cuman way of life. His favourite concubine was Aydua, an evil woman whom the Noblemen and prelates called "poisonous viper".

In 1289, they came to Zagreb. That was a very hard time for Zagreb and its citizens. Cumans took somebody's possessions—or life—every day for Aydua's amusement. Ladislaus ruled over Hungary, but Aydua ruled over Ladislaus. People never knew how to behave in her presence. She liked to gossip.

One day, one of her minions, to attract her attention, told her about a beautiful woman who'd lived in the neighbourhood some years ago.

"Nobody is more beautiful than I am," she said. "Find out everything you can about that family. Find the descendants. I don't want to see you until you bring me some news about that family. But work fast—I can't wait forever."

One nobleman came the next day and said, "I'm sorry, Your Majesty, but there is nobody from that family around. They all died or moved to Germany."

"Where in Germany? You knew that I would want to know that. You dare to come with incomplete information? Guard, throw him in the jail."

For a week or two, nothing happened. Then suddenly the Cuman's chieftain appeared in the palace looking for Aydua. When he found her, he said, "Collect your things. You are coming back home with me."

"But—"

"No buts. You are putting in the danger people who saved my life."

"But—"

"Guard, get her and her things. We are going back home immediately."

She left and was never seen again.

Ladislaus IV died in 1290. He was succeeding by Stephen the Posthumous, king of Hungary and Hrvatska from 1290 until 1301.

Stephen the Posthumous proclaimed himself the king of Hungary and Dalmatia, but there were some challengers to the throne: Rudolf of Germany; Andrew, duke of Slavonia;

and Mary, Ladislaus IV's sister and the wife of Charles I of Naples.

In general, that part of history had historical confusion. Hungary was fragmented into lots of countries, and different royal houses claimed throne.

The king was chosen on the proposal of the noblemen, barons, lords, prelates, and god knew who else.

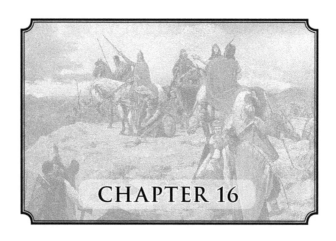

CHAPTER 16

NOVAK (PEASANT REBELLION)

Because of the constant need for the soldiers, the structure of nobility completely changed. Old nobility was abandoned; their property was taken and given to the new nobility. New nobility grew out of the powerful individuals who could, in the case of war, gather an army for the king.

Nobility behaved like they were masters of life and death for the poor peasants. They would burn whole villages if they weren't satisfied with the harvest. That was cause for the biggest peasant uprising in Europe. The peasants prepared for the war the best they could. They formed peasants' government in which they chose Matija Gubec, Ivan Pasanac, and Ivan Mogaić. The military captain was Iliya Gregurić. The war started in 1573 and ended after twelve days. On the first day, peasants had some success, but the next day the rebels couldn't resist the attack of Josip Turn, soldiers from Kostajnica, and professional German soldiers. They killed three thousand peasants and all leaders except Matija Gubec.

During the last few hours, when it was evident that they were losing the battle, Šime, Matija's neighbour, came close to him and said, "Come with me, Matija. I have a good hiding place in my house. Save yourself."

Everybody around him told him to hide and prepare another uprising. Finaly he accepted. He went with Šime to his cellar and that hiding place. In the night, he went out, found his nephew Ivan, and said to him, "Ivan, come with me. I don't trust this Šime, but he won't know anything about you. Come hide with me, and don't come out no matter what happens. You're young—save yourself."

The next morning Matija heard voices. That was Šime with a few German soldiers. Matija was dragged out of the hiding spot. They didn't expect anybody else to be in cellar and didn't look further. It was dark in the cellar, and they didn't notice Ivan.

Matija asked Šime, "Why are you doing this? Why didn't you let me die in the battle?"

"They promised to give me a baron's title and castle if I helped them to get you alive. For that price, I would sell my own mother." Ivan survived to tell this story.

Matija's punishment was horrible. He was dragged through the streets of Zagreb wearing a red-hot iron crown pinched with red-hot pincers. In the end, he was quartered.[13]

The hero from Zagorje died as a martyr, but he was still alive in the hearts of Hrvats and in a song.

There is no peasant, there is no hero,

Like Gubec Matija.

Šime didn't enjoy his award for a long time. Ten days after his treason, his new servants found him with his tongue and fingers cut off. He died twenty days afterwards from a fever.

---

[13] Cut into four parts.

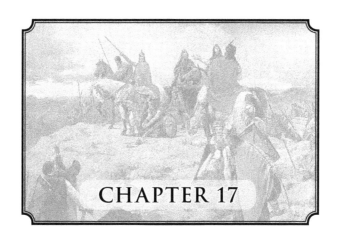

CHAPTER 17

IVEK'S DIARY (HIS WORDS)

My friends hid me until we were sure that nobody was looking for me anymore. Then we formed the court to interrogate and punish Šime.

He looked very surprised, asking what he had to do with Matija. He said that he offered to hide Matija, but Matija didn't accept, and he didn't know what Matija did and where he went.

One of the advisors asked him why the king gave him the castle and that big property. He said that he'd saved some money through the long period and that his father had left him some money as well. He'd bought the property from the owner. He thought that the owner was dead, but the owner had a son whom Šime didn't know. He was very surprised when the owner's son stood up and said that everything Šime had said was a lie, and he'd seen when leader of the group which had arrested Matija gave Šime the money. Šime didn't say a word after that, shaking all over.

The judge called me out as a witness, and I told how everything happened. The judge and the advisers went to the other room to talk about the case and bring the verdict.

When they came back, the judge said that they decided because of the treason, they'd cut off Šime's tongue. For taking money, they'd cut off all his fingers.

In 1526, during the reign of Louis II (1516–1526), Hungary and all the countries under Hungarian rule (including Hrvatska) became part of the Austrian Monarchy. Hrvatska was divided into parts in the Austrian Monarchy: Banovina Hrvatska, Slavonia, and Coastal Hrvatska ruled by Hungary, and Dalmatia under the rule of Venice.

For the Balkan Peninsula, that was the time the Turks showed up.

CHAPTER 18

TURKS

In 1371, in the battle on the River Marica, they defeated the Macedonian army. In 1389, in the battle in Kosovo, they defeated Serbia.

They attacked Hrvatska in 1493 for the Battle of Krbava. The war lasted one hundred years (1493–1593), though there wasn't constant fighting. The Turks had special war tactics. They first sent raiders to the chosen territory to rob and kill citizens. They were very cruel and bloodthirsty. The Turks didn't have to pay them; their award was the loot.

After them, the Ottoman army (the Turk's army—yanichars) would attack and occupy that territory. They had a special way to get warriors. They took the male children from each family in the occupied territories and sent them to military schools to learn warriors' skills and become soldiers. That was called danak u krvi.[14] There was a saying: "Becoming a Turk is worse than being born a Turk." To confront and stop Turkish advancing, part of the territory was taken from Hrvatska to be populated with soldiers. Soldiers could take a piece of land and bring their families there. That territory was called Krajina (Military Frontiers). It was taken from Hrvatska's territory and was under direct rule of the Austrian Monarchy.

The idea was that every soldier would fight harder if he was fighting for his family and his property. It worked, but Hrvatska became very small.

Because of that division of parts of Hrvatska, Marko's idea to connect all parts of former Hrvatska, Slavonia, and Dalmatia by forming small groups of dedicated men to keep their historical inheritance (language, culture, and customs) was very clever and important.

The Military Frontier was taken from Hrvatska, and it was ruled by the Austrian Monarchy.

In 1544, Turks broke through the Military Frontier and occupied Dubica, a town in Bosnia on the mouth of the River Una and the River Sava. Now Hrvats had to use the River Kupa as a defending wall. On the proposal of Hrvatska's Sabor and the recommendation of Zagreb's Bishop Nikola Olah, King Ferdinand I allowed Kaptol[15] to build the new fortress on the mouth of the Rivers Kupa and Sava. The new tower was built on the River Kupa, and the other one was

---

[14] Tax in blood.

[15] Part of the Zagfreb; at the centre, Hravatska's Catholic Church is situated.

on the River Sava. The walls of these towers were nine feet wide, and a third tower was built at the mouth of these two rivers with connecting walls seven feet high. The fortress was finished in 1552.

The first attack of Ottoman forces led by Hasan Pasha (Sultan's Murat III regent in Bosnia) happened in July 1591. The Turks were defeated, although they had the cannons. The second time Hasan Pasha surrounded Sisak was in July 1592. He kept Sisak under siege, using his war skills and far too powerful forces, but without success. The third time Hasan Pasha hit was in June 1593, with twenty thousand men. Defenders were in big danger. There were a lot of Hrvatska's warriors killed, and half of the tower on the River Sava was demolished. The Turks were ready for the main attack, but Sisak got reinforcements: Ban Tomo Erdedy with Hrvats, and Karlovac Andrija Auersperg with soldiers from the Military Frontier. The Turks suffered heavy losses. Hasan Pasha drowned in the River Kupa, and the sultan's nephew was killed.

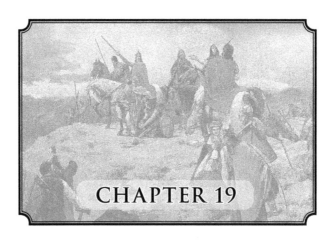

CHAPTER 19

DANKO'S DIARY

Danko was a soldier in the military squadron situated in Sisak to protect Hrvatska from the Turk attacks.

The Turks somehow managed to pass from Bosnia to Hrvatska during the night. They would silently raid one house, kill the men and kidnap the women, and disappear into the silence of the night.

One day Danko asked his captain for permission to visit his family in Zagreb. The captain let him go. Danko had a granddad in Zagreb and went to visit him as well. Granddad noticed that Danko was very sad and asked him what his problem was.

Danko said, "There is a girl in Sisak. I like her very much, and the Turks are coming into Sisak during the night through our fortress and kidnapping girls. I'm very afraid that they will kidnap her."

"Which fortress?" asked Granddad.

"We don't know."

"OK, wait here," said Granddad, and he disappeared. He came back with a bunch of paper with drawings of the fortresses. He spread out the papers on the table and said, "These are plans for your fortresses. There are a few underground passages I will show you now; there are two in each building. I will give you a list of builders engaged in this work, and you will find your traitor. Be very careful whom you taking to help you. Guard passages day and night because he will first go for the instructions."

Danko came back to Sisak and chose a group of soldiers he trusted. They secretly monitored all four entries. The plan was a success: they killed the Turks and the traitor.

Hrvatska's soldiers had now opened a free way for their raids in Bosnia.

The Turks tried a few times to get deeper into Europe. They managed twice to reach Vienna. The first attempt to win over Vienna was 1529. Turk Emperor Suleiman the Magnificent came with a big army and was heavily armed. The purpose of that attack was to help John Zapolja, a Hungarian nobleman, to become king of Hungary. Three years before the attack on Vienna, the Turks won the Battle of Mohacs. In that battle, the Hungarian king died, and the kingdom was in a civil war for the throne between King Ferdinand I and John Zapolja. The Turks were supporting John Zapolja.

Suleiman had cannons, between two hundred thousand and three hundred thousand yanitchars, and cavalry, but he was unlucky from the beginning. He started in Bulgaria, where there was a flood, and he was stopped because of mud. He lost his cannons. He lost his camels. Vienna had a well-organised defence and won.

The failure of the siege was the beginning of 150 years of bitter military tension and reciprocal attacks, culminating in a second siege of Vienna in 1683.

CHAPTER 20

HISTORICAL NOTES

It seems that a few diaries are missing.

After Rudolf, the next king was Mathias II (1608–1619). There was nothing written concerning Hrvatska.

Ferdinand II (1618–1625) enabled the population of the Military Frontier and put that part of Hrvatska under the direct rule of Vienna.

During the reign of Ferdinand III (1625–1657), nothing happened concerning Hrvatska.

Under Leopold II's (1657–1708) rule, Nikola Subic Zrinski and Krsto Frankopan were executed.

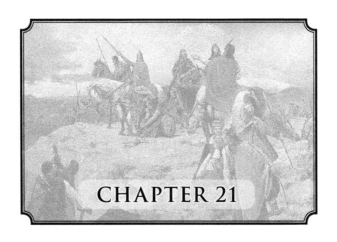

CHAPTER 21

ZDENKO

Habsburg's King Leopold I was more concerned with the fact that he had two free kingdoms in his country than a war with the Ottoman Empire. He wanted Hungary and Hrvatska to become part of his kingdom. He even conspired with the Turks. He offered them part of Hrvatska's territory for their support. Hrvatska's nobleman, Nikola Ŝ Zrinski, found out about that conspiracy, and he conspired with Hungarian nobles and European countries such as France to help free Hungary and Hrvatska from the Habsburgs. Unfortunately, he was killed by a wild boar His role in that conspiracy continued to His younger brother Petar, together with Hrvatska nobleman Krsto Frankopan.

They had a traitor in their circles, and King Leopold found out about the conspiracy. They were ordered to come to the emperor's court with promises that if they give up their uprising, they would be forgiven. That was a lie. The moment they came to Vienna, they were thrown in jail. The verdict was to cut off their heads.

The day before the execution of the sentence, they could write martyr letters to their wives. Nikola's letter was saved kept in Zagreb's archbishop archive. Here is the free translation of the part of that letter.

"My dear heart, don't be sad or cry because of this letter. By the end of God's tomorrow, at ten hours they will cut off my head, and your brother's as well. Today we asked each other for forgiveness. Now, with this letter, I am praying forgiveness from you.… I'm well prepared for death. I'm not afraid at all.… Don't be sad, this had to happen.

N. Mesto, before the last day of my life, 29 April at seven hours in the evening, year 1671. God bless my daughter, Aurora Veronica".

Groff Zrini Petar

jlim se Petar Zrinski oprašta od svoje
žene Katarine.

Peter Zrinski's letter to his wife

That was how the oldest Hrvatska aristocracy finished. The families had a lot of notable members who reached the position of ban.

Nikola ŝ Zrinski, Ban of Hrvatska (1542–1576)

Juraj V Zrinski, Ban of Hrvatska (1622–1626)

Nikola VII Zrinski, Ban of Hrvatska (1647–1664)

Petar Zrinski, Ban of Hrvatska (1665–1670)

Nikola (Subic) Zrinski, Ban of Dalmatia, Slavonia, and Hrvatska

Krsto Frankopan, Ban of Hrvatska (1482–1527)

Franjo Frankopan, Ban of Hrvatska (1536–1572)

Nikola Frankopan of Trzac, Ban of Hrvatska

They were fearless warriors who fought Turks in defence of Siget and Vienna. They fought through the centuries wherever was needed. Their families had properties all over Hrvatska Zrinski: Upper Kupa, Una, Bribir, Pedalj, Semidraz, Jamnicki Grad, Ozalj, and Frankopan. They had castles in Gorski Kotar, Severin on Kupa, Ribnik, Vasiljevo, Novi Vinodolski, Krk Island, Senj, Cetingrad, Trsat, and more. All of this was confiscated, and they families died out.

During the reign of Joseph I (1705–1711), there was nothing concerning Hrvatska.

Charles III (1711–1740) issued the document "Pragmatic Sanction" with what enabled female inheritance of the Austrian crown.

After the death of King Charles III in 1740, thanks to the "Pragmatic Sanction", the throne went to Maria Theresia. She introduced a lot of useful reforms in education and finance. She had sixteen children and tried to rule over Europe via the marital relations of her children. Her daughter was Maria Antonetta, who lost her life under the guillotine. Her daughter Maria Caroline was queen of Napoli, and Maria Amalia was the duchess of Parma. Her two sons were emperors of the Holy Roman Empire. She died in 1780. Maria Theresia divided Hrvatska into counties and created Hrvatska's Royal Council, but in 1779 it was all abolished.

Franz Joseph I (1848–1916) acknowledged the unity of Hrvatska, Slavonia Dalmatia, and Rijeka.

CHAPTER 22

NAPOLEON

After all these events, there was very little territory left of Hrvatska: Zagreb, with some land around it and a narrow strip of land in the Hrvatska's Primorje with the city Rijeka, which wished for independence and grew stronger.

Napoleon, in his warpath through Europe's countries after defeating the Austro-Hungarian army in the Battle of Austerlitz in 1806, received Venice, Istria, and the Dubrovnik Republic. He called those countries the Illyrian Provinces. He ruled until his debacle in 1814. The Habsburgs were incorporated into the Illyrian Provinces.

There were about twenty diaries for this period (twelfth through nineteenth century), mostly noting historical events and rulers. Marko left a group of his friends to take care of security and justice, but it seemed that their enemies were organised as well. Every Hrvatska conspiracy was uncovered, with the conspirators caught and punished. But our enemies failed to see the preparations of Atentate in Bosnia. In Bosnia and Herzegovina, the Hrvats didn't know anything about it, and they didn't take part in that event.

The nineteenth century was a time of big changes. There were scientific discoveries.

The steam machine
The locomotive
The telephone
The telegraph
The internal combustion engine
The rifle
Ironclad ships
Electricity and light bulbs
Photography

Capitalism made big step forward. Feudalism was dead. That brought new social classifications: the capitalists and the workers.

Hrvatska was left behind. Hrvatska was mainly vulnerable to Hungary, and Hungary supported its own progress. Hrvatska had small craft workshops which were usually family business.

But Hrvatska had always had very strong national awareness and eagerly reacted to the revival.

The actuator for Hrvatska's revival was Ljudevit Gay. His theory was that habitants on Balkan who had the same language were Illyrian descendants. He started with publishing *The Illyrian News* with little literary sublet Illyrian Danica.

CHAPTER 23

AUSTRIAN KINGS

Ferdinand I (1526–1564) tried to equalise Protestants with Christians, without success.

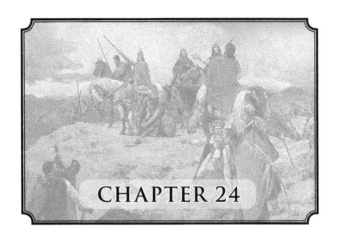

CHAPTER 24

DAMIR

The official language in Hrvatska was Latin. The peasants, citizens, and ordinary people spoke Hrvatska's language. The nobles usually spoke German or Hungarian. Hungary was pressing hard with its language. Ljudevit Gay started newspapers with the literary magazine *Danica* like an attachment. All young intellectuals and writers accepted a new way and started writing in Hrvatska's language. The Illyrian movement was the political movement. The aim was to unite nations on Balkan, especially Hrvatska, which was ransacked between Austria, Hungary, Venice, and the Ottoman Empire. Even political parties were formed on the basis of supporters and opponents.

The supporters were nationalists, and the opponents were Magyarons.

Hrvatska's nationalism worked on wider autonomy, but Hungarians pressed hard to suppress it. They did everything to discourage Magyaronise Hrvats, without success.

They introduced the Hungarian language in primary schools. This situation caused a lot of conflict. Hrvats had to hide the place and time of their meetings, but Magyarons somehow always found out where, and when the meeting was held, it would finish with a fight. In the end, the King forbade anything under the name IIlyr or Illyrian. That didn't stop Ljudevit Gay at all. The next day after the proclamation, the newspapers were issued under the title *Hrvatska's Newspaper,* and the literary adjacent was *Hrvatska Danica.*

The goal of the movement was to unite nations which had the same language and culture, and that was achieved.

A lot of writers were writing in Hrvatska's language. It was opened a lot of new libraries, but the Magyarons were a big nuisance.

Damir was very worried. They'd had that spy for too long. A lot of his friends were hurt in street conflicts. Some of them were in the hospital, and some of them ended up in prison.

He called everybody for the next meeting in the library. Two days after, he informed everybody and told them the different time and the day. Magyars showed up on the day he gave to the man he already suspected. He was watching every day. Ten days later, he repeated the same process with the same result. Next time when they had a meeting, everybody came except his suspect. The Magyars thought that he was a double spy, and they killed him.

Damir decided that it was time for him to retire and let his son Vitomir continue his work and his duties.

CHAPTER 25

VITOMIR

Vitomir was thrilled to take on that duty. It was time to prepare all that was needed for Sinjska Alka, and he loved that.

Sinjska Alka was the equestrian competition usually held annually (every first Sunday in August) since 1715 in the town Sinj, in Cetinska's Military Frontier, to celebrate the victory of about 1,300 Hrvats and Venetians defending against the Sinj and about 60,000 Turk yanichars.[16] The rules of the competition were codified in a statute from 1833, which promoted ethics and fair play. Rules were very strict. Participants must be members of local families of Sinj and Cetinska Krajina.[17] The whole community helped to make, conserve, restore, and reconstruct weapons, clothes, and

---

[16] Turk soldiers.
[17] Hrvatska's name for Cetinska's Military Frontier.

accessories for the tournament because everything must be as it was in the beginning of the eighteenth century when the competition started.

The competition had religious connotations and started as an appreciation for the Lady of Mercy because such a victory could be done only with her help.

The tournament was approved by the Austrian king, and the winner was awarded. Hungary tried to forbid the game but was unsuccessful.

Competition always started with the parade of all competitors, and it lasted for three days (Friday, Saturday, and Sunday). The allowed number of competitors was between eleven and seventeen.

The parade procession included the participants, the Alkars, the squires, Alajcaus, and the Alka master.

Alka squires were dressed in the traditional folk costume. They wore dark blue trousers, a white cotton shirt, and a black waistcoat richly adorned with silver buttons and filigree. On their heads they had red caps decorated with tassels. Around the waist, they had a silver belt with a sabre and gun tucked into it. On their feet, they wore domestically produced socks and opanke.[18]

Alkars wore a costume typical for knights. They wore dark blue trousers just like squires but embroidered with silver. Their shirt was white but embroidered with white linen on the back. Around the waist, they had wound around the

---

[18] Footwear made as a domestic product from narrow straps of cow leather.

waist a multicoloured band. They wore white gloves. On the heads they had a cylinder like a hat, and on their feet they wore black leather boots.

The horses were richly adorned as well.

The leader of the lancers was called Alajcaus and rode at the end of the procession.

Competitors raced three times. During the contest, knights rode horses at full gallop along the main street, aiming lances at an iron ring hanging on a rope.

The ring consisted of two rings connected with three bars. The smaller ring was in the centre of the bigger one. Connecting bars divided space between two rings into four sections plus the space in the middle. A hit through the canter gave three points. On the top in the bigger section between two bars was two points, and on the was two points. The two smallest sections down were one point each. At the end of three races, every competitor presented the sum of his points. If there were more competitors with the same number of points, they raced again until there was one with a bigger number of points.

One year, Austrian monarch Ferdinand I was present at the games, and he was so thrilled that he ordered every year winner get an award from his royal vault.

Alka is on the UNESCO List of Cultural Heritage.

Vitomir was sitting in the library and thinking about all that he had to organise and do. His friend Peter Jakupec pl[19]

---

[19] Noble.

entered the library out of breath. He had been friends with Vitomir for as long as he could remember. Vitomir had been coming to the castle with his dad, and later by himself, to cure the horses. The boy was always around and looking at what they were doing, but his mother was strongly against that. She was very happy when her husband decided to send the boy to Vienna for further education. She thought that the boy, far away in Vienna, would forget all about this common people, their language, and their habits.

Therefore, she was very disappointed when he said, "I'm going to visit Vitomir."

"I really don't know what you see so interesting in that common person."

"Sinjska Alka, Mother. Sinjska Alka," he said.

"Peasant's game, peasant's language, common friends," she murmured angrily.

But Peter didn't listen anymore. He simply said while going toward exit, "Bye, mother," and he was gone.

Vitomir was very happy to see him. "Peter!" he shouted. "My dear friend! When did you come home?"

"Vitomir!" shouted Peter at the same time. "I'm so glad that I found you here. Are you busy?"

"I will always find the time for you, no matter how busy I am. Did you finish your studies?"

"o," said Peter. "I have one year left, but my parents—well, I must be honest, it's not both, just Mother. She found out that I joined the Illyrian movement. Father came straight to Vienna and brought me home."

"If he is not the one who is against it, why did he come?" asked Vitomir.

"Oh, you don't know my mother. When she starts to complain because of something, the easiest way is to do something in connection with her problem, or else you will have to listen about it till you die."

"Why can't people look after their own business? The world is full of fools."

"But I didn't come to complain. I know that you are very busy with preparing everything for Alka. I came to see if I can help you.

"Oh, thank you very much," said Vitomir. "Like always, I don't know where to start. Let's go to my house. First, we must make the plans. You were always very good at making the plans."

When they reached Vitomir's house, Peter said, "Can we talk here? Is your house free of spies?"

"No spies here. We can talk freely. What is so urgent?"

"It's about your cousin Elisha. I'm in love with her, and she is in love with me. If Mother finds out about that, I wouldn't be able to guarantee Elisha's safety. I want to marry Elisha and then leave this country to one where these Hungarians don't have any influence."

Vitomir remembered when he saw Elisha for the first time. He thought she was a goddess. He would always think about her as a goddess or princess. Once, long ago when they were still kids, he'd called her a princess.

She looked him with fright in her eyes. "Who told you that? That is big secret. Somebody wants to kill me because of that."

"But I don't think, I don't …" stammered Vitomir.

"Please don't say that ever again."

Now, Vitomir said, "That's very good that you two are in love. She needs protection. Your mother is looking at her with a very strange expression on her face. I'm afraid that she somehow found the truth and could attack any time."

"What did she find out? What are you talking about?" said Peter.

"Oh, you don't know? Elisha didn't tell you anything?"

"Tell me what??"

"Let's check the room first. Check everywhere, because she is in deadly danger."

They checked everywhere and didn't find anything, but unfortunately they were standing in front of the fireplace, and Lea, who was in the room over theirs, heard the conversation.

Vitomir said, "Peter, Elisha is a princess, the descendant of the chieftain of our tribe when Hrvats were still in the old country, Snowy Mountain. She has a lot of enemies who want to kill her."

"Over my dead body," said Peter. "I must find a good hiding place for the two of us.

"That's Serbia," said Vitomir. "We Illyrians have a lot of good friends over there—young poets, writers, and scientists. They are all the supporters of our movement."

Eventually, Peter's father came home, and his wife started to complain immediately. He interrupted her. "Woman! I'm fed up with your Hungarianism and your snobbism. In this house, only Hrvatska's language from now on."

"But he didn't say even hello—just stormed out, took Silver, and off he went!" she continued complaining.

"Took Silver, and he is going to Sinj?" Boris repeated. "I'm going to Sinj as well." He grabbed the other horse and rode off.

When he reached Sinj, the tournament was already in progress.

Peter said to Vitomir, "Please keep quiet about the wedding. And for your information about where we are going to live, we are going to stay in Zadar. During these three years I spent in Vienna, I was playing piano in a very nice night bar. They liked me, and I was well paid. With that money, I bought the castle and surrounding estate in Zadar. We will change our names and surnames. You are the only person who will know our new names and address. Please don't give that information to anyone. Elisha's enemies are looking for her everywhere. They are very serious in their intention to kill her. When somebody asks what Elisha's plans are, Mother and I usually say that she will probably go to France or Germany, to learn how to work as a servant or maid."

Suddenly one uninvited guest crashed the gate. Leona pl Jakupec arrived. Boris was expecting something like that to happen, and he went early in the morning to visit the judge and tell him the story concerning his wife. The judge called two young police officers and told them that a lady was coming from Zagreb and was a dangerous criminal. They must follow her everywhere she went, and if they noticed anything unusual, they should arrest her on the spot. But she behaved nicely, with handshakes and kisses on the cheek to everyone, including Elisha.

When a waitress came with drinks, Lady Lea took the two glasses of sherry, one for Elisha and the other for herself, and two glasses of wine, one for Boris and the other for Peter. She secretly dropped one pill in each of them while offering the glasses to Boris and Peter.

The policemen were ready. They came close, and each of them took one of her hands. One of them removed the drinks, saying, "Leave the drink, my lady. It's not time for it yet. Come with us—we have to show you something."

A local chemist took the glasses somewhere, but he was back soon. He nodded his head and whispered, "Strychnine in one glass with cherry, and in both glasses with the wine."

She was trying to release her hands and somehow managed it. She was free, grabbed a knife, and jumped towards Elisha. "You are dead!" she said.

But Elisha grabbed the sabre from the table, used it skilfully, and ripped Lea's dress. "This time the dress. Next time the face."

Lea was so frightened that she let the policemen tie her hands again without a word, and she was taken out of the room She noticed Boris in the hole.

"I don't want to go anywhere, Boris. Help me! Where they are taking me?"

"Just go with them," he said. "They are good lads. They will give you something to calm you down. You're just tired. Everything will be OK when you wake up."

She started screaming again. "You're all fools, blind! Think! Which family has daughters so skilled in fencing? And I have powerful friends as well. You will be punished!. I belong to one very dangerous organisation of the paid killers. You will all die!"

Somebody from outside shot and killed her.

"I can't believe that my own mother wanted to poison me," said Peter.

"She's not your mother," said Boris.

"What?"

"I was very young when I met her, and she was a beauty. I fell for that, but I soon realised that she's not a good wife—and that she can be dangerous. One of the servants told me that she's there as a spy and is a killer, but he couldn't prove that. I completely lost interest in her and was rarely home. Soon I met a lovely girl, Rebecca, and fell in love with her. She loved me too. When she told me that she was pregnant, I was so happy, and I decided to send my present wife back from where she came from and marry Rebecca. Rebecca died during your birth. I became the happiest and unhappiest man in one day—I got you but lost her.

"I wrapped you up in a blanket and brought you home. I said to my wife that I found you on the doorstep of the house, and because I didn't have my own child and didn't want a child with her, I would adopt you. She started screaming that she would kill both of us, and I told her that I know a lot bad things about her. I wrote all that in a letter, which I gave to my advocate. If something bad happened to me or you, the advocate had instructions to open the letter and follow the instructions.

"That's why she was waiting till you finished your studies. She thought once when you were a lawyer, I would give all important documents to you, and she'd be able to get them. However, I was home as little as possible, and you were with Vitomir most of the time. I said to Vitomir's dad that my house was not healthy for my boy. I think he understood. I remember that because Peter was asking what kind of danger was in his house."

Now when Peter thought thinking about his childhood, he remembered a lot of occasions when he could be deadly hurt. On one occasion, his horse was very restless and didn't let anybody mount him. They called Damir, and he found a big thorn in the horse's leg. And there was that funny thing with the swing. His stepmother had brought a swing for him and Vitomir. Luckily his dad was home, and he said that he had to check that swing before they started using it. He found two loosened screws. He told them to check every part of that swing before using it. They did, and every time they found something wrong on it. Finaly his dad threw away the swing and told Peter to go to Vitomir's house to play because their house wasn't a healthy atmosphere.

Boris let the law take care of further actions. He sold all his possessions and disappeared. Only Vitomir knew that he was gone with his son in Zadar.

Peter said to Vitomir, Dear Vitomir, just give me the letter for your friends in Zadar. They are fighting for Slav's unity. I'm going for one year to Vienna. I want to finish my studies, and when I come back, I'm going to fight for that cause with full strength. I just need the connections.

"OK," said Vitomir, "that's great. I will give you three letters. One for Director Miho Klaic; he is from Dubrovnik. One for the Serbian poet Petar Preradovic. And one for the Slovene poet Stanko Vraz. You go now, and I will come to visit you, bring the letters, and tell you all what I know about them—their biographies and how reliable they are."

Ten days later, Vitomir showed up at Peter's house with the letters for his three friends and their written biographies.

> ***Dr. Miho Klaić.*** Born 19 August 1829 in Dubrovnik. Education: he finished primary school in Dubrovnik and secondary school in Dubrovnik and Livorno. (His family moved to Livorno.) After that, he went to the University in Padova, where he finished his PhD in mathematics in 1858.
>
> In Vienna, he passed the professor's exam in mathematics and physics. His first job was in the secondary school in Zadar, where he

joined the national party, whose main goal was to unite Dalmatia and Hrvatska. He had dangerous enemies amongst the taliyanash[20] and autonomash.[21]

Petar Preradović. Born in Gregoria (near Pitomaca) in 1818. He went to school in Grubisno Polje. His father was a military officer, and he put his son in military school. He very early started to write poems in German. He didn't know Hratska's language. He met Illyrians Ivan Mazuranic and Stanko Vraz and became an enthusiastic supporter of the movement. He learned Hrvatska's language as an adult and continued to write poems in that language.

Stanko Vraz. Born in the village of Cerovec, Stanko was one of most important figures of the Illyrian movement. He wrote poems and collected folk poems. He also translated foreign literature into Hrvatska's language. When he was in Samobor, he met the niece of his friend Ljudevit Gaj, and she became his muse. Vraz's most important work was collecting national Illyrian songs—songs from Stajerska, Kranjska, and Koruska.[22] These songs were the first

---

[20] Supporters for unity with Italy.
[21] Supporters of self-government
[22] Parts of Slovenia.

Slovene text in Gaj's Latin Alphabet. Stanko wrote a lot of poems in Slovene, but lots of them were never published. He also translated the works of Lord Byron and Adam Mickiewicz.

As the keeper of the national treasure, Vitomir had to travel a lot to Zagreb, Zadar, Zagreb, and Krk. On one of these trips, he met a sympathetic girl named Darinka. She was full of life and joy. His work was very hard, and he needed somebody who could make him laugh and forget the danger of his work. A few months after they met, they got married, but soon he became suspicious. She changed. He couldn't say in what way she changed, but she was different. She was still the joyful, childish girl he'd met, but she was different.

Then he suddenly realised she was too curious, asking things like did he know a lot of girls and had he been in love before. She tried to make it like the questioning of a jealous woman, but he sensed that very soon she would openly ask about Elisha. Then it happened. After returning from one of his travels to Zadar, he found Darinka sitting in the living room, waiting for him. She looked very angry.

"Did you meet your life's love? Are you happy now?" she asked.

"What are you talking about?" asked Vitomir.

"Don't think that I didn't find out about that pretty girl, that funny 'pretending to be a princess' Elisha, or whatever her name is."

Vitomir knew it wouldn't be good to fight because in anger, he could say something that could give her a clue about his whereabouts. He simply went out of the house for a long walk to calm himself down. When he came back, she was in the library writing the letter, which she quickly pushed under one book on the table, trying to hide it. He pretended as he didn't notice anything.

"Do you want your dinner now?" she asked.

"No, thank you. I have a lot to do—write a few letters, browse through today's newspapers. The most important thing is I have one book from an Illyrian supporter, and I must read it, edit it, and give it to the publisher to be published."

"You are busy," she said. "I leave you to it. I'm tired, and I'm going to sleep."

She exited the room, and he moved to sit at the table. She had left all stationery on the table. He noticed the blotting pad had changed recently, and he could read Darinka's last letter from the absorbent paper.

> I can't stand this anymore. Please get rid of him, or let me poison him. I spent so much time with him and couldn't find anything about that girl except what I've heard from servants. He is like an oyster. He doesn't talk, and he will never talk about her. I tried with anger and accusations today. He just vents out of the house.

Vitomir heard Darinka's steps through the hall. He quickly put the blotting pad where it should be and moved to the sofa with newspapers in his hands. Darinka collected her stuff and went out again, this time to the bedroom. Vitomir opened his safe and took out some paper and all his money. Then he wrote his testament. All that I possess, I'm leaving to my dear wife, Darinka." He quietly left the room, the house, and very probably the country too.

One night a month after his disappearance, they found Darinka dead in bed. During the investigation, it became obvious that some bad people thought that she was Elisha, and they'd killed her.

In 1840 the Illyrian movement moved from a cultural group to resisting the political demands of Hungary.

In 1843, by orders of Metternich, the use of the Illyrian name was forbidden. The movement simply changed the name to the Hrvatska movement. After the Hungarian revolution in Hrvatska, like the other countries in Austria, Hungary was introduced to Bach's absolutism, which introduced censure; abolished civil rights, the Hrvatska language, and the ban's council; and introduced the German language.

In 1851, after Octroyed's contribution, they introduced new absolutism, abolished civil liberties, introduced censure, and abolished the Hrvatska language and the ban's council.

In 1860, Hrvatska's Sabor brought three different opinions, which became the base for forming political parties in Hrvatska: unionists, nationalists, and Hrvatska's party of rights.

In 1867, Austria and Hungary made a settlement by which the name of the monarchy became the Austria-Hungarian Kingdom, and the countries under their ruling were divided into the countries of the St Steven Crown and the countries of the Austrian Monarchy.

Hungary had to make a similar settlement with the countries under her ruling.

Hrvatska wasn't satisfied with the settlement, and Eugen Kvaternik started a mutiny but was entrapped and killed.

For Hrvatska's ban, the king nominated Ivan Mazuranic. He ruled with the help of Hrvatska's National Party, but when Austria annexed Bosnia and Herzegovina, Mazuranic resigned, and Hungary was forced, against Hrvatska's will, Hungarian Khuen Hedervary to be ban. He used bribery, deterrence, and falsification of elections. Dissatisfaction with Hungarians grew stronger and caused lots of riots and inner conflict.

After the reaction and accusation in European countries, Hungary had to remove Khuen from the ban's position, but he became a minister in the Austrian government.

Such dissatisfaction had to result in an explosion. In Bosnia and Herzegovina, with the help of the Serbian organisation, the Black Hand, a group of young people, formed an organisation called Young Bosna. The members of that group decided to kill Archduke Franz Ferdinand during his visit to Sarajevo, the capital of Bosnia and Herzegovina.

Attentat was executed by Gavrilo Princip. He killed the archduke and his wife.

They doubted that all this was organised in Serbia, which in the meantime became a strong and independent country. Austria-Hungary declared war on Serbia, and that was the trigger for World War I. All Europe was in the war, and for first time in history, nations used tanks, airplanes, U-boats, and chemical warfare.

The war started on 28 July 1914 and finished on 11 November 1918. Estimates on the number of people killed were about nine million military people and about seven million civilians.

This war was a trigger for genocide later, and when combined with the people who died from the Spanish flu, the number came to fifty to one hundred million. That was the deadliest war ever.

Life in Hrvatska during that war was very hard. First, young boys and fathers of the families were taken to fight for Austria-Hungarian interests—what a paradox. Then Italians entered Hrvatska. Then came the starvation, and on the top of all this came the Spanish flu.

Hrvatska was decimated.

INDEPENDENCE AND UNITY

CHAPTER 26

YUGOSLAVIA

After the end of World War I in 1918 and after the Austria-Hungarian breakdown, Europe started tailoring new countries. In the first place, Hrvatska finally got its divided parts back (Dalmatia, Slavonia, Dubrovnik, Istria, and Krajina),[23] which was good. But on 1 December 1918, the kingdom of Slovene was formed, and Hrvatska and Serbia were under the rule of a Serbian king from the Karadjordjevic house, which wasn't so good. During the war, Slavic politicians were working on the idea of unity. They were present at all European conferences, presenting their ideas and plans for Croatia Radić, Serbia Pašić, and Dalmatia Trumbić.

They had very little in common, a similar language, and their habits were different. But the most important thing was

---

[23] Formerly the Military Frontier.

religion and the idea of how that union should look. Hrvatska had a dream about independence, and that dream lasted through the centuries. Serbia wanted to become a big, strong country, including all the Balkan countries under the rule of the Serbian king. In 1929 the name of country changed to the Kingdom of Yugoslavia, and that included Slovene, Hrvatsks, Serbia, Bosnia and Herzegovina, Montenegro, and Macedonia. They were like "the horns in the sac". Politicians had their doubts and awareness about the differences from the very beginning.

The Dalmatian politician Ante Trumbić became a prominent southern Slavic leader during the war, and he led the Yugoslav committee. Trumbić faced initial hostility from Serbian Prime Minister Nikola Pašić, who preferred an enlarged Serbia over a united Yugoslav state. But in the end, they agreed to a compromise with the Declaration at Corfu on 20 July 1917. The name of the country was declared the United State of Serbs, Hrvats, and Slovene.

CHAPTER 27

LITTLE JOKE

Yugoslavia is bordered by BRIGAMA:[24] Bulgaria, Romany, Italy, Greece, Albania, Madjarska,[25] and Austria.

Yugoslavia was very poor and behind its time. Three-quarters of the population were engaged in farming in a very primitive way; they were too poor to buy modern machinery. In the northern part of the country where mostly Hungarians lived, there were some bigger estates, but landowners were foreign and mostly Hungarian. The first action of the new Yugoslav state was to break up estates and dispose of foreigners.

Dalmatians were leaving the country in big numbers and moving to America. There was some manufacturing in Belgrade in some other major population centres.

---

[24] With worries.
[25] Hungary.

Politically, everything was still temporary. Nikola Pašić came out with the first proposal, but Regent Aleksandar Karadjordjević rejected it. He suggested that instead Nikola Pašic overtake the leader of his party, Stojan Protic. Then the Democratic Party came out with a highly centralised agenda, and a number of Croatan member moved to opposition.

On 20 June 1928, Serbian Deputy Punisa Racic shot at five members of Hrvatska'si Peasant Party. Two of them died on the spot, and leader of the party, Stjepan Radic, died two weeks after.

On 6 January 1929, King Aleksandar Djordjevic suspended the constitution, banned the political parties, took executive power, and changed the country's name to Yugoslavia. He proposed a new constitution and gave up his dictatorship in 1931.

Aleksandar attempted to create a centralised Yugoslavia. He decided to abolish Yugoslavia's historical regions and already had drawings for new boundaries of the provinces and banovinas.

Many politicians were jailed or under police surveillance. The flags of the other nations in the country were banned, as well as the communist idea and the party.

The king was assassinated in 1934, in Marseille during his visit to France. He was succeeded by his eleven-year-old son, Peter II, with his cousin Prince Paul as regent.

That was already the time of Hitler and Mussolini. Prince Paul submitted to the pressure of fascists, and he signed the Tripartite Pact with them, which caused wide revolt amongst the people. There were demonstrations all over the country. People came out on the streets shouting, "Better to fight than pact! Better grave then slave!"

On 6 April 1941, Germany attacked Yugoslavia, bombing Belgrade. King Peter II escaped to England. This started World War II.

CHAPTER 28

STELLA

Unfortunately, Hrvatska decided to join the Axis Powers (Germany and Italy), separate from Yugoslavia, and became the independent country Hrvatska.

Every nation in Yugoslavia had military troops.

Serbia had chetniks. Nedicevci and Hrvats had ustashe and domobrane. Everyone had military groups. They fought each other and all of them together fought partisans. Partisans were the only ones to fight the fascists. Fascists were evil monsters. They would kill one hundred innocent civilians for each killed German, and fifty innocent civilians for one wounded German soldier. They marked the Jews with a yellow ribbon with a big "J" on it, tying it around their arms. A lot of Jews were sent to concentration camps.

In Kragujevac, a town in Serbia, they brought students from classes in the schoolyard and kill them as revenge for the deaths of Germans soldiers. Serbian poet Deanna Mokimokis wrote a poem about it under the title "The Bloody Fairy Tale."

> It happened in the country of the peasants.
> On the hilly Balkan with a martyr's death
> Died the group of students in one day.

But all that made people very angry instead of scaring them. They said, "If I'm to die, better with a gun in my hand. Better to die fighting for my life than waiting to be killed." They joined the partisans and armed themselves by taking weapons from enemies. Soon small groups of partisans grew into the national army. They were all heroes.

But let's start from the beginning.

Here starts my history as well. Yes, I was born during the war. All I know about my birth is that the woman I called Mum was, in fact, my stepmother. She told me that for my life's security, nobody could know anything about my origin. All she told me was that my mother was her best friend and that she promised she would take good care of me.

At that time, we lived in Mostar, a beautiful town in Herzegovina situated on the River Neretva. Beside our house was the house where Italians had their kitchen, and believe it or not, that little girl Stella (that's me) was a welcome guest in the enemy's house nearly every day, enjoying good food.

Mostar was often bombarded. Behind our houses was Hill Bjelušine, which was full of caves where we hid during attacks. Unaware of the danger, I joyfully sang nursery rhymes and danced, amusing the other people hidden in the caves.

The Axis military operations were undertaken in seven major offensives. The first offensive was the attack on the Free Republic Uzice, a liberated territory in Western Serbia. They managed the reoccupied territory, but most partisans escaped to Bosnia.

A second offensive operated in three parts: Operation Southeast Hrvatska, Operation Ozren, and Operation Prijedor. They didn't manage to encircle the partisans, who retreated over Igman Mountain to Bosnia.

The third offensive was the Battle on Kozara.

The fourth offensive was the Battle for Wounded and Sick (Typhus), saving four thousand wounded soldiers. There, Tito performed a great tactical move. He ordered that the bridge over Neretva be destroyed and said the Youths Brigade should go over Prenj Mountain to Bosnia. The enemy thought they were all going to Bosnia and turned its forces in that direction. But during the night, partisans built a pontoon bridge over the River Neretva, and they passed to the other side of the river, out of the encirclement. There were chetniks waiting there to attack them, but the partisans defeated them.

The fifth offensive was the Battle on the River Sutjeska, where partisans were encircled. The partisan's commander, national hero Sava Kovacevic, called them to hit and break the circle. They jumped shouting, "Hooray!"

They ran and shot and ran and shot. A lot of them fell, but many more broke the circle and escaped. The Sava was killed, and Tito was injured. River Sutjeska was blood coloured. A lot of partisans were killed, but they broke the circle. They needed rest after such a heavy battle. A group of partisans from Mostar came home during the night and hid. One of them, called Haso, was from a family which didn't agree with his decision, especially his mother. They were trying to force him to give up. They would say, "That's a stupid idea. Those few tired, hungry, and unarmed men can't fight the German army. My dear son, you are so young. Your whole life is in front of you. Son, don't waste the best years of your life."

His dad would usually add, "Listen to your mother, son."

One evening his sister invited her boyfriend to come to her house for dinner. Her boyfriend was a German officer. After dinner, they sat on the balcony with a glass of wine and made small talk. Between other topics, they were talking about war as well.

The next morning, Haso was arrested. After a few hours of interrogation and torture, he told them everything he knew, including the hiding places of the other partisans. When they couldn't get anything else from him, they let him go in the hope that they would find out more by following him. But he killed himself. Very disappointed, the Germans sent the rest of the family to a concentration camp. Nobody came back.

The sixth offensive was the protection of the Adriatic Coast after Italy's capitulation.

The seventh offensive was called Descent on Drvar. The enemy had information that Tito was in one of the caves above Drvar.[26]. They sent a troop of parachutists to Drvar with a photo of Tito and the order to kill him. The operation was unsuccessful.

Eventually, the war finished. The good people won, and there were songs and celebration everywhere. My stepmother came out of the house looking for me. Our neighbour Kana Micar, whose husband was ustaša, a war criminal, started shouting at her.

"You whore! Are you happy now? You'll probably take all my properties, you communists. You are the thieves, all of you!"

My stepmother didn't listen to her anymore. She was just thinking about how she didn't have any reason for happiness because the only person who could make her happy wouldn't come back ever again. Her dear husband had been killed in the war by the war criminal Schulze. All that was left that could make her happy was revenge.

Shulze killed three members of her family: her husband, her brother, and her brother-in-law. He also killed my mother, my father, and my granny.

My stepmother brought me to Punat, a town on the island of Krk, where the parents of my dad lived. She left me with them for a while. I spent three years with my Nona and Nono.[27] Those three years were probably the happiest years of

---

[26] A town in the north-west part of Bosnia.

[27] That's how they say Granny and Granddad in Punat.

my life. My Granddad took me everywhere. We first visited all my cousins, and there was good number of them. He took me swimming, but I liked it the most when we sat at the doorstep and he read fairy tales to me. He had big book of fairy tales which would take me to a magical world of dragons, witches, princes, and princesses. That was my world, my life, my dreams. In the stories, I always knew who was nice and noble and from whom one should run away.

But nothing is forever. When I was six years old, my stepmother brought me back to Mostar because it was time to start school. I didn't have any problem with the school and my studies, but socialising with the other children was a different story. I was quiet and very shy; it was hard to make a friend. I had cousins in the United States, and they regularly sent money for me and lovely toys. I wasn't short of anything except love. My stepmother loved me, but she was very strict, and I was afraid of her. I secretly called her the Steel Lady.

Mostar was a little town with about 17,000 citizens. It was a mixed population but mostly Muslims. Lots of them gave their lives for our freedom. Fifteen of them were named war heroes.

In the war, everything was destroyed. The whole country was in ruins and in need for rebuilding and reconstruction—roads, railways, factories, houses. The nation was full of enthusiasm and jest. Young people formed Youths Brigades to work on constructing new roads and railways. They were working for free with songs on their lips and in their hearts.

Then in 1948, there was conflict with Stalin and Russia. Stalin was for centralism, and he thought he would rule over all of Eastern Europe. Tito was the president and didn't agree with that.

We were one political country, communist, but it wasn't bad. All schools were for free. Tito's motto was, "Learn, learn, and just learn."

Before the war, stepmother had finished just primary school, and she was working in a factory. Now she decided to do some courses, and then she got a job in an office. All the money she get, she gave to private investigators in the hope that they would find Shulze. I had my own money because every month, money was sent to me from America. She never touched that money it was only for my needs. She was very strict, and when it was time for school, she took me from Granny and Granddad and brought back to Mostar to live with her. She punished me for every mischief.

My granddad never even shouted at me.

When I was in my last of secondary school, she said that she must talk to me. She made coffee for us, and we sat in chairs on the balcony. She was quiet for a while, and then she said, "What do you think about archaeology? Would you like to study?"

I was speechless and had never thought about that profession, but I liked the idea. "Why?" I said.

Without a word, she opened a big box that was lying on the table between us. "Have a look," she said.

I looked, and there were a lot of diaries.

"These are the diaries of your ancestors, from the moment they came to Balkan until the unity of southern Slavs in the kingdom of Serbs, Hrvats, and Slovene. I'm just finishing the period 1918–1945. Your duty is to describe the events after 1945. And you should also find and punish Shulze. I will tell you the whole story when I have more time. First read the diaries, and then I will explain everything to you."

I said OK and went back to my studies. I nearly forgot all about them.

Then my stepmother died, and I met Maximillian Morgenstern. He told me the whole story and asked me, "Did you read the diaries?"

I was ashamed. "No," I admitted.

"Read them, and I will come again."

I didn't read them, and he didn't come back.

In the country, it looked like everything was good, but not completely. Hrvatska's tourism was blooming. Hrvatska had a lot of emigrants from the United States and other foreign countries, and so Hvatska was getting lots of money going through central bank in Belgrade. Hrvatska's politicians, intellectuals, and youth couldn't agree with that movement (Hrvatska's Spring). A lot of them ended up in the jail.

Concerning the working class, you were working class if you had a job and some family in the villages to help you with food (some vegetable and some meat). You could live nicely. But new rachis showed up. (They usually would say that they were worthy. Were the rest of us unworthy? Ordinary people weren't completely satisfied.

Then the leadership in Serbia became crazy, wanting to introduce centralism in the country, a Stalinist system. When they were turned down by Slovenia and Hrvatska, they let Slovene go and attacked Hrvatska. That was the Homeland War, which Hrvatska won.

Sometime before the Homeland War, I met a strange man, Inspector Detective Varvik. I met him in the shop.

He said to me, "Hello, Miss Stella. Just the woman I was looking for. It is not easy to get you; you are rarely home. Sorry—I should first introduce myself. I am Police Inspector Varvik, and I have a few questions for you."

I said, "Why don't we go to my apartment? I'll make coffee or tea, and we can sit and talk."

"Great idea," said Varvik.

He helped me put my shopping in the car, and we went to my modern, spacious adobe. While sitting comfortably on the sofa, he took a photo from his pocket and asked if I knew the man in the photo.

"Of course, I know him. That's my old friend. Poor man. He was very good with the old scripts—hieroglyphics and Glagolits. He is not Jewish but has a Jewish name and surname. He managed to escape from the concentration camp, but that war criminal Schulze killed his wife and child. He is not the same man anymore. The last time I saw him a few months ago, we were talking. In the middle of a sentence, he stopped, looked over my shoulder, and said, 'That's Schulze.' I turned around, but nobody was there. I turned back to him, but he was running after his enemy. I tried to contact him again, and I have his phone number, but there's no answer. Has something happened to him? Why this inquiry? Is he hurt?"

"He is dead," said the inspector. "It could be suicide, but we must be sure about that. Please, if you remember anything that could help us, call me. Here is my business card."

I took the card and promised to call him if I found out something new, and he left. I sat for a while thinking about the past. The past was very important for an archaeologist.

Schulze was a war criminal guilty for all mass killings and high crimes in Balkan during World War II. He was involved in killing students and civilians as revenge for killed and wounded Germans (similar the one in Kragujevac which Serbian poet Desanka Maksimovic wrote about in her poem "A Bloody Fairytale").

I didn't read the diaries, but I did try to find Shulze. I had been trying to find him all these years, but nobody really knew him except Morgenstern, and now he was dead. I had my doubts but no proof.

Tomorrow was important day. Hrvatska was recognised as a sovereign, independent nation. Tomorrow I was going to my park, where I'd meditate and find my inner peace.

Late at night, somebody knocked at my door. It was Inspector Varvik.

He said, "I was visiting your neighbour. He's going to Argentina—moving. He already sent all his possessions, he told me. I'm afraid we won't solve our case. Well, I'll be going home now. Good night."

"Good night," I said. "And don't believe all that is told."

The next day, when I woke up, I had my breakfast, got dressed, and started to celebrate independence in my own way. I was going to my dearest park to enjoy freedom. When I got there and sat on one of the benches, I closed my eyes to meditate. I heard a voice.

"Good morning, Stella."

It was Professor Vojkovic, better known as Schulze. He was holding a gun in his right hand. The spider had come out from his hole.

"I'm leaving this country. I decided to have a little talk with you before that. I really don't know why you meddled in this story, but I want to enlighten you on a few things. The basic story you know, and you read the diaries. How did you get them, anyway?"

"From my stepmother," I said.

"But you gave me a copy. Are the original diaries written in the Glagolits, or did you do that?"

"I did," I said. "Firstly, I couldn't give the you original because there are things in them which you are not allowed to know. Secondly, I knew that was the best way to get you out from the hole where you were hiding. The original diaries are written in Latin."

"That's what I thought. The thing you don't know is that Nevena was pregnant with Rudolph. You probably are asking yourself how I know that. You see, after Rudolph's execution, his son Fabrizio entered in all Yagelich's houses servants (just a few of them) who were working for us. Their duty was to listen and tell us everything that happened in their houses.

One servant heard when Nevena said to Almer, 'Almer, I can't marry you.'

"'What is that now?' asked Almer. 'It's nationality again. is it? Or you don't love me anymore.'

"'None of it,' said Nevena. 'I'm pregnant with Rudolph's child. I love you every day more and more. You are one noble soul, Almer.'

"'We will give child to someone who can't have children. You won't even see it if you don't want to.' When the time came, Nevena brought to the world a boy and a girl. The boy's name was Slaven, and the girls' was Lilia. When he heard about the pregnancy, Fabrizio sent a message to his granny.

"'Come straight away to the Snowy Mountains. Nevena is pregnant. The child is Mintz.'

"Granny's name was Marta. She was very happy thinking that Nevena would keep the children, and she would have grandchildren.

"The children were born on 15 January—I don't know the year. They were beautiful children, both like real Yagelovichs, except when they were angry. Then something strange happened with their eyes.

"Granny told the children about their parents and added that their mother didn't love them. Slaven was devastated. He was enchanted with his mother and secretly followed her whenever he could. Lilia hated her. Marta hated her before because of Rudolph's death, but now she was crazy with hatred. She went to the church and gave the oath of hatred to kill all Yagelovichs. That crazy race to kill and destroy started. First was Gordan.

"I just don't know how Yagoda escaped," said Vojkovic.

"But I know," I said. "When she met that soldier in Knin, she knew that was a trap because Gordan would never send a message by a person she didn't know. When she was close to Makarska, she exchanged her beautiful horse for dirty clothes, cut her beautiful black hair, and continued towards Makarska as a beggar. Nobody paid attention to her."

Schulze continued. "We managed perfectly with Nikola and Hope, but then came Marko. Marko was our evil spirit. We were in every bad thing that happens to Hrvatska: death of Duke Mislav, Duke Zdeslav, King Zvonimir, the deaths of Hope and Nikola, the peasant rebellion, Subic-Zrinski. Everything and everybody except Yagoda and Marko. As for pl. Jakupec, we sent that woman to his house. She was ordered through the noble Boris to enter Dammar's house. But when became noble herself, she didn't want to socialise with Damir because he was common. In the end, we had to kill her because she was screaming to everyone that she belonged to the association of killers and that they would come to save her. We didn't pay attention to events in Bosnia, and that was a fatal mistake. Because of that mistake, today you are celebrating Independence Day."

"Yes," I said, "nine hundred years after Zvonimir's curse."

"I don't know what happened with Marta the Youngest," murmured Schulze.

"I don't know what happened to her, but I know what happened to her granddaughter. Recently I went to the police archive to see something about a witch hunt in Zagreb. I found out that in Zagreb, 132 females were accused of witchcraft, and only three were let go. While I was reading the names, one name caught my eye: "Marta—burnt on the stake'. She was killing the men, using a knife and shouting, 'Marko, greetings from Marta.'"

"The poor, crazy creature," said Schulze. But tell me something. What kind of person are you? Meddling in other people's business, and you are celebrating this day. You don't even know who you are."

"I know very well who I am," I said proudly. "I am a human, and to be a human is the best nationality to me."

"Well, that's your problem. My problem is that I'm the last Mintz. I had a chance to have a child with a good woman, and I destroyed it. When I killed Lisa, I found out that she was pregnant. That was my child. Bah, it doesn't matter. I'm rich, and I'm going to Argentina. I will find a young, beautiful girl and start a new generation of Mintzes."

"Why did you kill her?"

"She was plotting against me. I just wanted to scare her, but she jumped towards me, and a bullet hit her. Believe it or not, I loved her. I was surprised myself when I realised that. I couldn't believe that I would be have that feeling. I also felt sadness, loss, emptiness … Never mind—let's finish this." He straitened his arm, ready to shoot.

Two things happened at the same time. I saw the dog jump on him and bite his arm. Varvick started running and shooting. Schulze was hit in the lungs and was dying. He looked at the dog and then me, finally understanding.

"Yagelovich?"

I said yes.

"Which line?"

"Nevena's. Yagoda … Lisa."

"Lisa," he whispered with sadness. "She knew that I know Glagolits, always drawing some …"

Suddenly he stopped talking. "Did she know Glagolits?" he asked.

I said, "No, nobody except me. But her house was full of those messages. She learned how they looked but not what they meant. She drew them when she was stressed."

"But how, why?" Then he stopped again and started laughing. He died laughing.

"Why did he laugh?" Varvik asked.

"He just remembered who else was drawing and writing little notes."

"Case solved," said Varvik. "Now we must find the owners of all the things he was trying to take to Argentina."

"Be careful. If you see a beautiful ring with a big emerald, don't touch it!"

"Yours?" he asked.

"Probably, but I don't want it."

"So, Mogenstern was your granddad."

"No, he was a friend. He is Marko's descendant. He came to Zagreb in Lisa's house because that was one of the places from where Jewish were moving to America. He was with the other ten families hidden in a cellar, in an unnoticeable hiding place. He was just going to the kitchen to get some food when he heard from the hall orders in German language. He had just enough time to hide in a wardrobe. That was Schulze with two German soldiers. Schulze broke the apartment's door, went straight to the kitchen, and said to Lisa, 'You communist.'

"Her mum started crying, begging him to leave Lisa alone. She was repeating, 'She's not a communist.'

"'You're too noisy,' he said, and he shot her.

"Morgenstern didn't dare let any noise out because of the families downstairs, but he saw him very well. The rest you know."

"Madam Stella," said Varvik, "I'm going to open the boxes which Shulze left to check what is in them. Would you mind coming with me? I will take one policeman with us to help."

I accepted the invitation. I was surprised by Ola's behaviour. She was between Varvik and me all the time, showing mistrust and caution.

When the policeman joined us, we entered the warehouse and started opening the boxes. All the boxes were empty. In the last one we found a note: "Look for treasure in the enchanted cave." I think if the policeman wasn't there, he would have killed me on the spot. His face showed so much anger and hatred. Ola growled and came closer to me. I realised that Varvik was looking for that treasure for himself and not for the owners—and that I would live until he found that treasure. I tried to remember why that sounded so familiar, but the more I thought about that name, the less I remembered.

One night I had strange dream. I was crying, and I remembered my mother so clearly. Then an old lady sat beside me. She looked at me with her lovely dark blue eyes, and then she hugged me gently and said, "Don't cry, Stella."

Then I woke up. I was still under the impression of that dream, which looked so realistic that I was looking around in the hope that I would find old lady.

"Where is the boy?"

The question surprised me more than them because until then, nobody had mentioned a boy. I had hidden a memory in one part of my mind, a story about an old lady who was a real person, and an imagined boy. I knew if I stopped forcibly pushing myself to remember, the memory would come.

I decided to go to Punat. They found a passage under the church made in mosaic. I had to go see that. While working on the excavation, I forgot everything else.

Suddenly Varvik showed up. "Where did you disappear to? I was looking everywhere for you. What are you doing, anyway? We have a different excavation to dig."

"No problem," I said. "Find the excavation, and I will dig."

"Ha-ha, very funny," he said. "Come on. We have more important work to do"

I agreed. I had a feeling that my memories were awakening and that I was on the edge of remembering them. I collected my things and went back to Zagreb to prepare myself for a long travel. The solution was in White Mountain—I was sure of that. I packed and made a few very important phone calls. By the next morning, we were off.

I fell asleep on the train, and suddenly the old lady showed up. She sat on my bed and kissed both my eyes. Then she said, "Close your eyes, my love. I will tell you a story about a beautiful princess."

The story started like all fairy tales did.

"Once upon a time long, long ago, there was a beautiful princess. Her eyes were like a blue sky, and her smile was as warm and friendly as a sunny day. Her walk was soft and soundless like a puma's, but she was ready to jump quickly if somebody wanted to attack her. She was always faster and invincible.

"She lived with her family in a beautiful country full of joy and happiness. Unfortunately, one day a bad man came and did bad things to her. She survived and her body's injures healed, but her soul was hurt forever. She hid her pain well. Soon after, a prince from a nearby country came and proposed. He had already proposed once before, and she'd declined his proposal, but now she accepted.

"After marriage, she and her husband moved to the Snowy Mountain, which was cold and dark. But in the spring, it changed to a beautiful place: birds chirping, and flowers of every kind. She was already pregnant and gave a birth to boy and a girl. She gave up the children on their birthday, but her heart cried bloody tears. She liked that mountain very much, with clear lakes and flowers everywhere.

"While wandering around, she found a cave hidden behind big trees; the entry was covered by bushes and flowers. She found it by accident, trying to reach one beautiful flower which was a bit too high for her. She lost her balance and slid into the cave. That cave became her place for remedy. It looked as if nobody had ever been inside. The next time she visited the cave, she found it full of flowers. She thought about silly messages regarding dangerous paths for her, and she knew that somebody was following her. She had noticed that a while ago, and she knew in her heart that the person was a friend. She needed a friend because her husband was a beast. He'd hated her from the moment she hadn't accepted his first proposal. He was simply waiting for the moment for revenge, and the case with Mintz served him well. He beat her regularly, taking care that he hit only the covered parts of her body. Everybody thought he was perfect husband.

"She wanted to know who that friend was, and so one day when she knew he was behind her, she turned around and saw a boy—her son. Her heart pounded with joy and happiness, but he disappeared."

In that moment I woke up, but now I remembered the whole story. The old lady was my granny from Punat. She'd told me just one story when I was three years old. It was this story. It wasn't make-believe but was the truth.

The first thing to do was to make a phone call. Then I went to the bathroom, had a shower, dressed, and called Varvik. He answered after the first ring, and it looked like he was waiting by the phone.

"We must go to Poland," I said. "Book the first flight to Krakow and meet me at the airport."

"Why? Did something happen?" he asked.

"I remembered something that will bring us to the enchanted cave."

"Great," he said. "Are you going to tell me the whole story?"

"My granny told me all about Nevena and described the enchanted cave and how to find it. I hope that the surroundings haven't changed a lot."

"Pray to God," said Varvik.

In that moment came the call for travellers in Krakow to aboard. We booked a hotel and went for a little walk through Krakow to see the sights. After that, we had dinner, and I went in my room to have a good rest because I knew that tomorrow would be very tiring. Varvik went his own way.

The next morning, we started very early. We prepared everything that was needed for safe mountain hiking, including a tent and camping gear. Then we took the bus to Zakopane. From Zakopane, we continued walking up to Tatre Mountain. I walked very slowly, looking for the signs I'd heard from my granny.

I noticed the first sign. The path divided into two paths, and she chose left path. Then I started counting steps. After thirty-five steps, I stopped and looked around

"What are you looking for?" asked Varvik.

"The wild rose," I said, and in that moment I saw it.

I ran towards the wild rose and found two strong sticks. With them I pushed the rose on the side, and the entry to the cave showed up. I entered, and Varvik entered after me.

"Is that it?" he asked, holding a gun in my direction. "Hurry up now. Where did Shulze hide the stolen goods? What did the old witch tell you? Is there a little room somewhere? Quickly tell me where the hiding place is—I'm in a hurry. I can't believe that you didn't see through me. You are very naïve."

He heard a female voice behind him. "There you are wrong, dear Schmidt.".

He looked like he'd seen a ghost. He was shaking, and the gun fell from his hand to the ground. He stammered, "Lissa?"

In that moment, three policemen entered the cave, arrested him, and took away.

"How did you call him? I asked.

"Schmidt," Mother said. "He was with Shulze in all his crimes."

"I hugged and kissed my mother. "But what happened with you? I thought, and even he thought, that you were dead, that he'd killed you."

"Oh, I had a good friend. Albert, come out now."

Out of the back of the cave came a tall, slim, very old man. Albert was an undercover English spy. He had orders to save Lissa and kill Shulze. Albert said. "When Shulze shot Lissa. I told him that she was dead. He didn't turn around to check—he just ran out of the room. I was connected with a group of soldiers from England, and they organised our escape. Your mother was in England until recently. Then she said that her daughter was in danger, and she must go to Hrvatska to save her."

Albert didn't want to let her go alone. First he contacted Interpol and found out that Shulze was dead, and that I was in a hunt with Smith. "We organised this trap and got him. We took everything that Shulze hid here. The owners already got back their valuables."

"Mother, Albert, are you going with me to Zagreb? Not to visit but to stay?"

"Of course," said Mother.

When we came to Zagreb and entered my house, I opened the door. In the sitting room was Ola in her bed, with three little puppies jumping around her.

Mother stepped towards her, and she growled gently.

"What's her name?" asked Mother.

I said, "Wolverine, but I call her Ola."

Mother was quiet for a while, thinking about something. Then she said, "Imagine the coincidence. Hrvatska got independence nine hundred years after Zvonimir's death."

ABOUT THE BOOK

This book is about the Croats coming to Balkan Peninsula, their fight to survive, and family revenge.